SELECTED *Poems*

BOOKS BY GWENDOLYN BROOKS

Poetry
A Street in Bronzeville
Annie Allen
Bronzeville Boys and Girls
The Bean Eaters
Selected Poems
In the Mecca
Riot
Family Pictures
Aloneness
Aurora
The Tiger Who Wore White Gloves: Or, What You Are You Are
Beckonings
Primer for Blacks
To Disembark
The Near Johannesburg Boy and Other Poems
Gottschalk and the Grand Tarantelle
Winnie
Children Coming Home
Blacks

Fiction
Maud Martha

Autobiography
Report from Part One
Report from Part Two

gwendolyn brooks

SELECTED *Poems*

HARPER**PERENNIAL** MODERN**CLASSICS**

NEW YORK • LONDON • TORONTO • SYDNEY

HARPER**PERENNIAL** ● MODERN**CLASSICS**

FIRST PERENNIAL CLASSICS EDITION PUBLISHED 1999.
FIRST HARPER PERENNIAL MODERN CLASSICS EDITION PUBLISHED 2006.

The Library of Congress has catalogued the Perennial Classics edition as follows:
   Brooks, Gwedolyn.
     [Poems. Selections]
     Selected poems / Gwendolyn Brooks.— 1st Perennial Classics ed.
       p. cm.
    ISBN 0-06-093174-4
    1. African Americans—Poetry. I. Title.
    PS3503.R7244A6 1999
    811'.54—dc21   98-54645

ISBN-10: 0-06-088296-4 (pbk.)
ISBN-13: 978-0-06-088296-9 (pbk.)

21 22 23 LSC 30 29 28 27 26 25 24 23

To Bob and Alice Cromie
and to the memory of Frank Brown.

Acknowledgments

Thanks are due the following: *Common Ground, Poetry, Cross-Section 1945, Harper's Magazine,* Franklin McMahon, *Country Beautiful, Beloit Poetry Journal*

Contents

ANNIE ALLEN

THE BEAN EATERS

NEW POEMS

SELECTED Poems

A STREET IN
BRONZEVILLE

A Street in Bronzeville

to David and Keziab Brooks

kitchenette building

We are things of dry hours and the involuntary plan,
Grayed in, and gray. "Dream" makes a giddy sound, not strong
Like "rent," "feeding a wife," "satisfying a man."

But could a dream send up through onion fumes
Its white and violet, fight with fried potatoes
And yesterday's garbage ripening in the hall,
Flutter, or sing an aria down these rooms

Even if we were willing to let it in,
Had time to warm it, keep it very clean,
Anticipate a message, let it begin?

We wonder. But not well! not for a minute!
Since Number Five is out of the bathroom now,
We think of lukewarm water, hope to get in it.

the mother

Abortions will not let you forget.
You remember the children you got that you did not get,
The damp small pulps with a little or with no hair,
The singers and workers that never handled the air.
You will never neglect or beat
Them, or silence or buy with a sweet.
You will never wind up the sucking-thumb
Or scuttle off ghosts that come.
You will never leave them, controlling your luscious sigh,
Return for a snack of them, with gobbling mother-eye.

I have heard in the voices of the wind the voices of my dim
      killed children.
I have contracted. I have eased
My dim dears at the breasts they could never suck.
I have said, Sweets, if I sinned, if I seized
Your luck
And your lives from your unfinished reach,
If I stole your births and your names,
Your straight baby tears and your games,
Your stilted or lovely loves, your tumults, your marriages, aches,
      and your deaths,
If I poisoned the beginnings of your breaths,
Believe that even in my deliberateness I was not deliberate.
Though why should I whine,
Whine that the crime was other than mine?—
Since anyhow you are dead.
Or rather, or instead,
You were never made.

But that too, I am afraid,
Is faulty: oh, what shall I say, how is the truth to be said?
You were born, you had body, you died.
It is just that you never giggled or planned or cried.

Believe me, I loved you all.
Believe me, I knew you, though faintly, and I loved, I loved you
All.

southeast corner

The School of Beauty's a tavern now.
The Madam is underground.
Out at Lincoln, among the graves
Her own is early found.
Where the thickest, tallest monument
Cuts grandly into the air
The Madam lies, contentedly.
Her fortune, too, lies there,
Converted into cool hard steel
And right red velvet lining;
While over her tan impassivity
Shot silk is shining.

hunchback girl: she thinks of heaven

My Father, it is surely a blue place
And straight. Right. Regular. Where I shall find
No need for scholarly nonchalance or looks
A little to the left or guards upon the
Heart to halt love that runs without crookedness

Along its crooked corridors. My Father,
It is a planned place surely. Out of coils,
Unscrewed, released, no more to be marvelous,
I shall walk straightly through most proper halls
Proper myself, princess of properness.

a song in the front yard

I've stayed in the front yard all my life.
I want a peek at the back
Where it's rough and untended and hungry weed grows.
A girl gets sick of a rose.

I want to go in the back yard now
And maybe down the alley,
To where the charity children play.
I want a good time today.

They do some wonderful things.
They have some wonderful fun.
My mother sneers, but I say it's fine
How they don't have to go in at quarter to nine.
My mother, she tells me that Johnnie Mae
Will grow up to be a bad woman.
That George'll be taken to Jail soon or late
(On account of last winter he sold our back gate).

But I say it's fine. Honest, I do.
And I'd like to be a bad woman, too,
And wear the brave stockings of night-black lace
And strut down the streets with paint on my face.

the ballad of chocolate Mabbie

It was Mabbie without the grammar school gates.
And Mabbie was all of seven.
And Mabbie was cut from a chocolate bar.
And Mabbie thought life was heaven.

The grammar school gates were the pearly gates,
For Willie Boone went to school.
When she sat by him in history class
Was only her eyes were cool.

It was Mabbie without the grammar school gates
Waiting for Willie Boone.
Half hour after the closing bell!
He would surely be coming soon.

Oh, warm is the waiting for joys, my dears!
And it cannot be too long.
Oh, pity the little poor chocolate lips
That carry the bubble of song!

Out came the saucily bold Willie Boone.
It was woe for our Mabbie now.
He wore like a jewel a lemon-hued lynx
With sand-waves loving her brow.

It was Mabbie alone by the grammar school gates.
Yet chocolate companions had she:
Mabbie on Mabbie with hush in the heart.
Mabbie on Mabbie to be.

the preacher: ruminates behind the sermon

I think it must be lonely to be God.
Nobody loves a master. No. Despite
The bright hosannas, bright dear-Lords, and bright
Determined reverence of Sunday eyes.

Picture Jehovah striding through the hall
Of His importance, creatures running out
From servant-corners to acclaim, to shout
Appreciation of His merit's glare.

But who walks with Him?—dares to take His arm,
To slap Him on the shoulder, tweak His ear,
Buy Him a Coca-Cola or a beer,
Pooh-pooh His politics, call Him a fool?

Perhaps—who knows?—He tires of looking down.
Those eyes are never lifted. Never straight.
Perhaps sometimes He tires of being great
In solitude. Without a hand to hold.

Sadie and Maud

Maud went to college.
Sadie stayed at home.
Sadie scraped life
With a fine-tooth comb.

She didn't leave a tangle in.
Her comb found every strand.

Sadie was one of the livingest chits
In all the land.

Sadie bore two babies
Under her maiden name.
Maud and Ma and Papa
Nearly died of shame.

When Sadie said her last so-long
Her girls struck out from home.
(Sadie had left as heritage
Her fine-tooth comb.)

Maud, who went to college,
Is a thin brown mouse.
She is living all alone
In this old house.

the independent man

Now who could take you off to tiny life
In one room or in two rooms or in three
And cork you smartly, like the flask of wine
You are? Not any woman. Not a wife.
You'd let her twirl you, give her a good glee
Showing your leaping ruby to a friend.
Though twirling would be meek. Since not a cork
Could you allow, for being made so free.

A woman would be wise to think it well
If once a week you only rang the bell.

of De Witt Williams on his way to Lincoln Cemetery

He was born in Alabama.
He was bred in Illinois.
He was nothing but a
Plain black boy.

Swing low swing low sweet sweet chariot.
Nothing but a plain black boy.

Drive him past the Pool Hall.
Drive him past the Show.
Blind within his casket,
But maybe he will know.

Down through Forty-seventh Street:
Underneath the L,
And Northwest Corner, Prairie,
That he loved so well.

Don't forget the Dance Halls—
Warwick and Savoy,
Where he picked his women, where
He drank his liquid joy.

Born in Alabama.
Bred in Illinois.
He was nothing but a
Plain black boy.

Swing low swing low sweet sweet chariot.
Nothing but a plain black boy.

the vacant lot

Mrs. Coley's three-flat brick
Isn't here any more.
All done with seeing her fat little form
Burst out of the basement door;
And with seeing her African son-in-law
(Rightful heir to the throne)
With his great white strong cold squares of teeth
And his little eyes of stone;
And with seeing the squat fat daughter
Letting in the men
When majesty has gone for the day—
And letting them out again.

The Sundays of Satin-Legs Smith

Inamoratas, with an approbation,
Bestowed his title. Blessed his inclination.

He wakes, unwinds, elaborately: a cat
Tawny, reluctant, royal. He is fat
And fine this morning. Definite. Reimbursed.

He waits a moment, he designs his reign,
That no performance may be plain or vain.
Then rises in a clear delirium.

He sheds, with his pajamas, shabby days.
And his desertedness, his intricate fear, the
Postponed resentments and the prim precautions.

Now, at his bath, would you deny him lavender
Or take away the power of his pine?
What smelly substitute, heady as wine,
Would you provide? life must be aromatic.
There must be scent, somehow there must be some.
Would you have flowers in his life? suggest

Asters? a Really Good geranium?
A white carnation? would you prescribe a Show
With the cold lilies, formal chrysanthemum
Magnificence, poinsettias, and emphatic
Red of prize roses? might his happiest
Alternative (you muse) be, after all,
A bit of gentle garden in the best
Of taste and straight tradition? Maybe so.
But you forget, or did you ever know,
His heritage of cabbage and pigtails,
Old intimacy with alleys, garbage pails,
Down in the deep (but always beautiful) South
Where roses blush their blithest (it is said)
And sweet magnolias put Chanel to shame.

No! He has not a flower to his name.
Except a feather one, for his lapel.
Apart from that, if he should think of flowers
It is in terms of dandelions or death.
Ah, there is little hope. You might as well—
Unless you care to set the world a-boil
And do a lot of equalizing things,
Remove a little ermine, say, from kings,
Shake hands with paupers and appoint them men,
For instance—certainly you might as well
Leave him his lotion, lavender and oil.

Let us proceed. Let us inspect, together
With his meticulous and serious love,
The innards of this closet. Which is a vault

Whose glory is not diamonds, not pearls,
Not silver plate with just enough dull shine.
But wonder-suits in yellow and in wine,
Sarcastic green and zebra-striped cobalt.
With shoulder padding that is wide
And cocky and determined as his pride;
Ballooning pants that taper off to ends
Scheduled to choke precisely.
                              Here are hats
Like bright umbrellas; and hysterical ties
Like narrow banners for some gathering war.

People are so in need, in need of help.
People want so much that they do not know.

Below the tinkling trade of little coins
The gold impulse not possible to show
Or spend. Promise piled over and betrayed.

These kneaded limbs receive the kiss of silk.
Then they receive the brave and beautiful
Embrace of some of that equivocal wool.
He looks into his mirror, loves himself—
The neat curve here; the angularity
That is appropriate at just its place;
The technique of a variegated grace.

Here is all his sculpture and his art
And all his architectural design.
Perhaps you would prefer to this a fine

Value of marble, complicated stone.
Would have him think with horror of baroque,
Rococo. You forget and you forget.

He dances down the hotel steps that keep
Remnants of last night's high life and distress.
As spat-out purchased kisses and spilled beer.
He swallows sunshine with a secret yelp.
Passes to coffee and a roll or two.
Has breakfasted.
                        Out. Sounds about him smear,
Become a unit. He hears and does not hear
The alarm clock meddling in somebody's sleep;
Children's governed Sunday happiness;
The dry tone of a plane; a woman's oath;
Consumption's spiritless expectoration;
An indignant robin's resolute donation
Pinching a track through apathy and din;
Restaurant vendors weeping; and the L
That comes on like a slightly horrible thought.

Pictures, too, as usual, are blurred.
He sees and does not see the broken windows
Hiding their shame with newsprint; little girl
With ribbons decking wornness, little boy
Wearing the trousers with the decentest patch,
To honor Sunday; women on their way
From "service," temperate holiness arranged
Ably on asking faces; men estranged
From music and from wonder and from joy

But far familiar with the guiding awe
Of foodlessness.
                    He loiters.
                              Restaurant vendors
Weep, or out of them rolls a restless glee.
The Lonesome Blues, the Long-lost Blues, I Want A
Big Fat Mama. Down these sore avenues
Comes no Saint-Saëns, no piquant elusive Grieg,
And not Tschaikovsky's wayward eloquence
And not the shapely tender drift of Brahms.
But could he love them? Since a man must bring
To music what his mother spanked him for
When he was two: bits of forgotten hate,
Devotion: whether or not his mattress hurts:
The little dream his father humored: the thing
His sister did for money: what he ate
For breakfast—and for dinner twenty years
Ago last autumn: all his skipped desserts.

The pasts of his ancestors lean against
Him. Crowd him. Fog out his identity.
Hundreds of hungers mingle with his own,
Hundreds of voices advise so dexterously
He quite considers his reactions his,
Judges he walks most powerfully alone,
That everything is—simply what it is.

But movie-time approaches, time to boo
The hero's kiss, and boo the heroine
Whose ivory and yellow it is sin

For his eye to eat of. The Mickey Mouse,
However, is for everyone in the house.

Squires his lady to dinner at Joe's Eats.
His lady alters as to leg and eye,
Thickness and height, such minor points as these,
From Sunday to Sunday. But no matter what
Her name or body positively she's
In Queen Lace stockings with ambitious heels
That strain to kiss the calves, and vivid shoes
Frontless and backless, Chinese fingernails,
Earrings, three layers of lipstick, intense hat
Dripping with the most voluble of veils.
Her affable extremes are like sweet bombs
About him, whom no middle grace or good
Could gratify. He had no education
In quiet arts of compromise. He would
Not understand your counsels on control, nor
Thank you for your late trouble.
                                        At Joe's Eats
You get your fish or chicken on meat platters.
With coleslaw, macaroni, candied sweets,
Coffee and apple pie. You go out full.
(The end is—isn't it?—all that really matters.)

            And even and intrepid come
            The tender boots of night to home.

Her body is like new brown bread
Under the Woolworth mignonette.

Her body is a honey bowl
Whose waiting honey is deep and hot.
Her body is like summer earth,
Receptive, soft, and absolute . . .

Negro Hero

to suggest Dorie Miller

I had to kick their law into their teeth in order to save them.
However I have heard that sometimes you have to deal
Devilishly with drowning men in order to swim them to shore.
Or they will haul themselves and you to the trash and the fish
    beneath.
(When I think of this, I do not worry about a few
Chipped teeth.)

It is good I gave glory, it is good I put gold on their name.
Or there would have been spikes in the afterward hands.
But let us speak only of my success and the pictures in the
    Caucasian dailies
As well as the Negro weeklies. For I am a gem.
(They are not concerned that it was hardly The Enemy my fight
    was against
But them.)

It was a tall time. And of course my blood was
Boiling about in my head and straining and howling and
    singing me on.

Of course I was rolled on wheels of my boy itch to get at the
      gun.
Of course all the delicate rehearsal shots of my childhood
      massed in mirage before me.
Of course I was child
And my first swallow of the liquor of battle bleeding black air
      dying and demon noise
Made me wild.

It was kinder than that, though, and I showed like a banner my
      kindness.
I loved. And a man will guard when he loves.
Their white-gowned democracy was my fair lady.
With her knife lying cold, straight, in the softness of her sweet-
      flowing sleeve.
But for the sake of the dear smiling mouth and the stuttered
      promise I toyed with my life.
I threw back!—I would not remember
Entirely the knife.

Still—am I good enough to die for them, is my blood bright
      enough to be spilled,
Was my constant back-question—are they clear
On this? Or do I intrude even now?
Am I clean enough to kill for them, do they wish me to kill
For them or is my place while death licks his lips and strides to
      them
In the galley still?

(In a southern city a white man said
Indeed, I'd rather be dead;

Indeed, I'd rather be shot in the head
Or ridden to waste on the back of a flood
Than saved by the drop of a black man's blood.)

Naturally, the important thing is, I helped to save them, them
    and a part of their democracy.
Even if I had to kick their law into their teeth in order to do
    that for them.
And I am feeling well and settled in myself because I believe it
    was a good job,
Despite this possible horror: that they might prefer the
Preservation of their law in all its sick dignity and their knives
To the continuation of their creed
And their lives.

Gay Chaps at the Bar

gay chaps at the bar

> . . . and guys I knew in the States, young
> officers, return from the front crying and
> trembling. Gay chaps at the bar in Los
> Angeles, Chicago, New York . . .
>
> Lieutenant William Couch
> in the South Pacific

We knew how to order. Just the dash
Necessary. The length of gaiety in good taste.
Whether the raillery should be slightly iced
And given green, or served up hot and lush.
And we knew beautifully how to give to women
The summer spread, the tropics, of our love.
When to persist, or hold a hunger off.
Knew white speech. How to make a look an omen.
But nothing ever taught us to be islands.
And smart, athletic language for this hour
Was not in the curriculum. No stout
Lesson showed how to chat with death. We brought
No brass fortissimo, among our talents,
To holler down the lions in this air.

still do I keep my look, my identity . . .

Each body has its art, its precious prescribed
Pose, that even in passion's droll contortions, waltzes,
Or push of pain—or when a grief has stabbed,
Or hatred hacked—is its, and nothing else's.
Each body has its pose. No other stock
That is irrevocable, perpetual
And its to keep. In castle or in shack.
With rags or robes. Through good, nothing, or ill.
And even in death a body, like no other
On any hill or plain or crawling cot
Or gentle for the lilyless hasty pall
(Having twisted, gagged, and then sweet-ceased to bother),
Shows the old personal art, the look. Shows what
It showed at baseball. What it showed in school.

my dreams, my works, must wait till after hell

I hold my honey and I store my bread
In little jars and cabinets of my will.
I label clearly, and each latch and lid
I bid, Be firm till I return from hell.
I am very hungry. I am incomplete.
And none can tell when I may dine again.
No man can give me any word but Wait,
The puny light. I keep eyes pointed in;
Hoping that, when the devil days of my hurt
Drag out to their last dregs and I resume
On such legs as are left me, in such heart
As I can manage, remember to go home,

My taste will not have turned insensitive
To honey and bread old purity could love.

looking

You have no word for soldiers to enjoy
The feel of, as an apple, and to chew
With masculine satisfaction. Not "good-by!"
"Come back!" or "careful!" Look, and let him go.
"Good-by!" is brutal, and "come back!" the raw
Insistence of an idle desperation
Since could he favor he would favor now.
He will be "careful!" if he has permission.
Looking is better. At the dissolution
Grab greatly with the eye, crush in a steel
Of study—Even that is vain. Expression,
The touch or look or word, will little avail.
The brawniest will not beat back the storm
Nor the heaviest haul your little boy from harm.

piano after war

On a snug evening I shall watch her fingers,
Cleverly ringed, declining to clever pink,
Beg glory from the willing keys. Old hungers
Will break their coffins, rise to eat and thank.
And music, warily, like the golden rose
That sometimes after sunset warms the west,
Will warm that room, persuasively suffuse

That room and me, rejuvenate a past.
But suddenly, across my climbing fever
Of proud delight—a multiplying cry.
A cry of bitter dead men who will never
Attend a gentle maker of musical joy.
Then my thawed eye will go again to ice.
And stone will shove the softness from my face.

mentors

For I am rightful fellow of their band.
My best allegiances are to the dead.
I swear to keep the dead upon my mind,
Disdain for all time to be overglad.
Among spring flowers, under summer trees,
By chilling autumn waters, in the frosts
Of supercilious winter—all my days
I'll have as mentors those reproving ghosts.
And at that cry, at that remotest whisper,
I'll stop my casual business. Leave the banquet.
Or leave the ball—reluctant to unclasp her
Who may be fragrant as the flower she wears,
Make gallant bows and dim excuses, then quit
Light for the midnight that is mine and theirs.

the white troops had their orders but the Negroes looked like men

They had supposed their formula was fixed.
They had obeyed instructions to devise

A type of cold, a type of hooded gaze.
But when the Negroes came they were perplexed.
These Negroes looked like men. Besides, it taxed
Time and the temper to remember those
Congenital iniquities that cause
Disfavor of the darkness. Such as boxed
Their feelings properly, complete to tags—
A box for dark men and a box for Other—
Would often find the contents had been scrambled.
Or even switched. Who really gave two figs?
Neither the earth nor heaven ever trembled.
And there was nothing startling in the weather.

firstly inclined to take what it is told

Thee sacrosanct, Thee sweet, Thee crystalline,
With the full jewel wile of mighty light—
With the narcotic milk of peace for men
Who find Thy beautiful center and relate
Thy round command, Thy grand, Thy mystic good—
Thee like the classic quality of a star:
A little way from warmth, a little sad,
Delicately lovely to adore—
I had been brightly ready to believe.
For youth is a frail thing, not unafraid.
Firstly inclined to take what it is told.
Firstly inclined to lean. Greedy to give
Faith tidy and total. To a total God.
With billowing heartiness no whit withheld.

"God works in a mysterious way"

But often now the youthful eye cuts down its
Own dainty veiling. Or submits to winds.
And many an eye that all its age had drawn its
Beam from a Book endures the impudence
Of modern glare that never heard of tact
Or timeliness, or Mystery that shrouds
Immortal joy: it merely can direct
Chancing feet across dissembling clods.
Out from Thy shadows, from Thy pleasant meadows,
Quickly, in undiluted light. Be glad, whose
Mansions are bright, to right Thy children's air.
If Thou be more than hate or atmosphere
Step forth in splendor, mortify our wolves.
Or we assume a sovereignty ourselves.

love note
I: Surely

Surely you stay my certain own, you stay
My you. All honest, lofty as a cloud.
Surely I could come now and find you high,
As mine as you ever were; should not be awed.
Surely your word would pop as insolent
As always: "Why, of course I love you, dear."
Your gaze, surely, ungauzed as I could want.
Your touches, that never were careful, what they were.
Surely—But I am very off from that.
From surely. From indeed. From the decent arrow

That was my clean naiveté and my faith.
This morning men deliver wounds and death.
They will deliver death and wounds tomorrow.
And I doubt all. You. Or a violet.

love note
II: flags

Still, it is dear defiance now to carry
Fair flags of you above my indignation,
Top, with a pretty glory and a merry
Softness, the scattered pound of my cold passion.
I pull you down my foxhole. Do you mind?
You burn in bits of saucy color then.
I let you flutter out against the pained
Volleys. Against my power crumpled and wan.
You, and the yellow pert exuberance
Of dandelion days, unmocking sun:
The blowing of clear wind in your gay hair;
Love changeful in you (like a music, or
Like a sweet mournfulness, or like a dance,
Or like the tender struggle of a fan).

the progress

And still we wear our uniforms, follow
The cracked cry of the bugles, comb and brush
Our pride and prejudice, doctor the sallow
Initial ardor, wish to keep it fresh.
Still we applaud the President's voice and face.

Still we remark on patriotism, sing,
Salute the flag, thrill heavily, rejoice
For death of men who too saluted, sang.
But inward grows a soberness, an awe,
A fear, a deepening hollow through the cold.
For even if we come out standing up
How shall we smile, congratulate: and how
Settle in chairs? Listen, listen. The step
Of iron feet again. And again wild.

ANNIE ALLEN

Notes from the Childhood and the Girlhood

the parents: people like our marriage
Maxie and Andrew

Clogged and soft and sloppy eyes
Have lost the light that bites or terrifies.

There are no swans and swallows any more.
The people settled for chicken and shut the door.

But one by one
They got things done:
Watch for porches as you pass
And prim low fencing pinching in the grass.

Pleasant custards sit behind
The white Venetian blind.

Sunday chicken

Chicken, she chided early, should not wait
Under the cranberries in after-sermon state.
Who had been beaking about the yard of late.

Elite among the speckle-gray, wild white
On blundering mosaic in the night.
Or lovely baffle-brown. It was not right.

You could not hate the cannibal they wrote
Of, with the nostril bone-thrust, who could dote
On boiled or roasted fellow thigh and throat.

Nor hate the handsome tiger, call him devil
To man-feast, manifesting Sunday evil.

old relative

After the baths and bowel-work, he was dead.
Pillows no longer mattered, and getting fed
And anything that anybody said.

Whatever was his he never more strictly had,
Lying in long hesitation. Good or bad,
Hypothesis, traditional and fad.

She went in there to muse on being rid
Of relative beneath the coffin lid.
No one was by. She stuck her tongue out; slid.

Since for a week she must not play "Charmaine"
Or "Honey Bunch," or "Singing in the Rain."

the ballad of late Annie

Late Annie in her bower lay,
Though sun was up and spinning.

The blush-brown shoulder was so bare,
Blush-brown lip was winning.

Out then shrieked the mother-dear,
"Be I to fetch and carry?
Get a broom to whish the doors
Or get a man to marry."

"Men there were and men there be
But never men so many
Chief enough to marry me,"
Thought the proud late Annie.

"Whom I raise my shades before
Must be gist and lacquer.
With melted opals for my milk,
Pearl-leaf for my cracker."

throwing out the flowers

The duck fats rot in the roasting pan,
And it's over and over and all,
The fine fraught smiles, and spites that began
Before it was over and all.

The Thanksgiving praying's away with the silk.
It's over and over and all.
The broccoli, yams and the bead-buttermilk
Are dead with the hail in the hall,
     All
Are dead with the hail in the hall.

The three yellow 'mums and the one white 'mum
Bear to such brusque burial
With pity for little encomium
Since it's over and over and all.

Forgotten and stinking they stick in the can.
And the vase breath's better and all, and all.
And so for the end of our life to a man,
Just over, just over and all.

"do not be afraid of no"

"Do not be afraid of no,
Who has so far so very far to go":

New caution to occur
To one whose inner scream set her to cede, for softer lapping
        and smooth fur!

Whose esoteric need
Was merely to avoid the nettle, to not-bleed.

Stupid, like a street
That beats into a dead end and dies there, with nothing left to
        reprimand or meet.

And like a candle fixed
Against dismay and countershine of mixed

Wild moon and sun. And like
A flying furniture, or bird with lattice wing; or gaunt thing,
        a-stammer down a nightmare neon peopled with condor,
        hawk and shrike.

To say yes is to die
A lot or a little. The dead wear capably their wry

Enameled emblems. They smell.
But that and that they do not altogether yell is all that we know
      well.

It is brave to be involved,
To be not fearful to be unresolved.

Her new wish was to smile
When answers took no airships, walked a while.

"pygmies are pygmies still, though percht on Alps"
—Edward Young

But can see better there, and laughing there
Pity the giants wallowing on the plain.
Giants who bleat and chafe in their small grass,
Seldom to spread the palm; to spit; come clean.

Pygmies expand in cold impossible air,
Cry fie on giantshine, poor glory which
Pounds breast-bone punily, screeches, and has
Reached no Alps: or, knows no Alps to reach.

The Anniad

Think of sweet and chocolate,
Left to folly or to fate,
Whom the higher gods forgot,
Whom the lower gods berate;
Physical and underfed
Fancying on the featherbed
What was never and is not.

What is ever and is not.
Pretty tatters blue and red,
Buxom berries beyond rot,
Western clouds and quarter-stars,
Fairy-sweet of old guitars
Littering the little head
Light upon the featherbed.

Think of ripe and rompabout,
All her harvest buttoned in,
All her ornaments untried;
Waiting for the paladin
Prosperous and ocean-eyed

Who shall rub her secrets out
And behold the hinted bride.

Watching for the paladin
Which no woman ever had,
Paradisaical and sad
With a dimple in his chin
And the mountains in the mind;
Ruralist and rather bad,
Cosmopolitan and kind.

Think of thaumaturgic lass
Looking in her looking-glass
At the unembroidered brown;
Printing bastard roses there;
Then emotionally aware
Of the black and boisterous hair,
Taming all that anger down.

And a man of tan engages
For the springtime of her pride,
Eats the green by easy stages,
Nibbles at the root beneath
With intimidating teeth.
But no ravishment enrages.
No dominion is defied.

Narrow master master-calls;
And the godhead glitters now
Cavalierly on his brow.

What a hot theopathy
Roisters through her, gnaws the walls,
And consumes her where she falls
In her gilt humility.

How he postures at his height;
Unfamiliar, to be sure,
With celestial furniture.
Contemplating by cloud-light
His bejewelled diadem;
As for jewels, counting them,
Trying if the pomp be pure.

In the beam his track diffuses
Down her dusted demi-gloom
Like a nun of crimson ruses
She advances. Sovereign
Leaves the heaven she put him in
For the path his pocket chooses;
Leads her to a lowly room.

Which she makes a chapel of.
Where she genuflects to love.
All the prayerbooks in her eyes
Open soft as sacrifice
Or the dolour of a dove.
Tender candles ray by ray
Warm and gratify the gray.

Silver flowers fill the eves
Of the metamorphosis.

And her set excess believes
Incorruptibly that no
Silver has to gape or go,
Deviate to underglow,
Sicken off to hit-or-miss.

Doomer, though, crescendo-comes
Prophesying hecatombs.
Surrealist and cynical.
Garrulous and guttural.
Spits upon the silver leaves.
Denigrates the dainty eves
Dear dexterity achieves.

Names him. Tames him. Takes him off.
Throws to columns row on row.
Where he makes the rifles cough,
Stutter. Where the reveille
Is staccato majesty.
Then to marches. Then to know
The hunched hells across the sea.

Vaunting hands are now devoid.
Hieroglyphics of her eyes
Blink upon a paradise
Paralyzed and paranoid.
But idea and body too
Clamor "Skirmishes can do.
Then he will come back to you."

Less than ruggedly he kindles
Pallors into broken fire.
Hies him home, the bumps and brindles
Of his rummage of desire
Tosses to her lap entire.
Hearing still such eerie stutter.
Caring not if candles gutter.

Tan man twitches: for for long
Life was little as a sand,
Little as an inch of song,
Little as the aching hand
That would fashion mountains, such
Little as a drop from grand
When a heart decides "Too much!"—

Yet there was a drama, drought
Scarleted about the brim
Not with blood alone for him,
Flood, with blossom in between
Retch and wheeling and cold shout,
Suffocation, with a green
Moist sweet breath for mezzanine.

Hometown hums with stoppages.
Now the doughty meanings die
As costumery from streets.
And this white and greater chess
Baffles tan man. Gone the heats

That observe the funny fly
Till the stickum stops the cry.

With his helmet's final doff
Soldier lifts his power off.
Soldier bare and chilly then
Wants his power back again.
No confection languider
Before quick-feast quick-famish Men
Than the candy crowns-that-were.

Hunts a further fervor now.
Shudders for his impotence.
Chases root and vehemence,
Chases stilts and straps to vie
With recession of the sky.
Stiffens: yellows: wonders how
Woman fits for recompense.

Not that woman! (Not that room!
Not that dusted demi-gloom!)
Nothing limpid, nothing meek.
But a gorgeous and gold shriek
With her tongue tucked in her cheek,
Hissing gauzes in her gaze,
Coiling oil upon her ways.

Gets a maple banshee. Gets
A sleek slit-eyed gypsy moan.

Oh those violent vinaigrettes!
Oh bad honey that can hone
Oilily the bluntest stone!
Oh mad bacchanalian lass
That his random passion has!

Think of sweet and chocolate
Minus passing-magistrate,
Minus passing-lofty light,
Minus passing-stars for night,
Sirocco wafts and tra la la,
Minus symbol, cinema
Mirages, all things suave and bright.

Seeks for solaces in snow
In the crusted wintertime.
Icy jewels glint and glow.
Half-blue shadows slanting grow
Over blue and silver rime.
And the crunching in the crust
Chills her nicely, as it must.

Seeks for solaces in green
In the green and fluting spring.
Bubbles apple-green, shrill wine,
Hyacinthine devils sing
In the upper air, unseen
Pucks and cupids make a fine
Fume of fondness and sunshine.

Runs to summer gourmet fare.
Heavy and inert the heat,
Braided round by ropes of scent
With a hypnotist intent.
Think of chocolate and sweet
Wanting richly not to care
That summer hoots at solitaire.

Runs to parks. November leaves
All gone papery and brown
Poise upon the queasy stalks
And perturb the respectable walks.
Glances grayly and perceives
This November her true town:
All's a falling falling down.

Spins, and stretches out to friends.
Cries "I am bedecked with love!"
Cries "I am philanthropist!
Take such rubies as ye list.
Suit to any bonny ends.
Sheathe, expose: but never shove.
Prune, curb, mute: but put above."

Sends down flirting bijouterie.
"Come, oh populace, to me!"
It winks only, and in that light
Are the copies of all her bright
Copies. Glass begets glass. No

Populace goes as they go
Who can need it but at night.

Twists to Plato, Aeschylus,
Seneca and Mimnermus,
Pliny, Dionysius . . .
Who remove from remarkable hosts
Of agonized and friendly ghosts,
Lean and laugh at one who looks
To find kisses pressed in books.

Tests forbidden taffeta.
Meteors encircle her.
Little lady who lost her twill,
Little lady who lost her fur
Shivers in her thin hurrah,
Pirouettes to pleasant shrill
Appoggiatura with a skill.

But the culprit magics fade.
Stoical the retrograde.
And no music plays at all
In the inner, hasty hall
Which compulsion cut from shade.—
Frees her lover. Drops her hands.
Shorn and taciturn she stands.

Petals at her breast and knee . . .
"Then incline to children-dear!

Pull the halt magnificence near,
Sniff the perfumes, ribbonize
Gay bouquet most satinly;
Hoard it, for a planned surprise
When the desert terrifies."

Perfumes fly before the gust,
Colors shrivel in the dust,
And the petal velvet shies,
When the desert terrifies:
Howls, revolves, and countercharms:
Shakes its great and gritty arms:
And perplexes with odd eyes.

Hence from scenic bacchanal,
Preshrunk and droll prodigal!
Smallness that you had to spend,
Spent. Wench, whiskey and tail-end
Of your overseas disease
Rot and rout you by degrees.
—Close your fables and fatigues;

Kill that fanged flamingo foam
And the fictive gold that mocks;
Shut your rhetorics in a box;
Pack compunction and go home.
Skeleton, settle, down in bed.
Slide a bone beneath Her head,
Kiss Her eyes so rash and red.

Pursing lips for new good-byeing
Now she folds his rust and cough
In the pity old and staunch.
She remarks his feathers off;
Feathers for such tipsy flying
As this scarcely may re-launch
That is dolesome and is dying.

He leaves bouncy sprouts to store
Caramel dolls a little while,
Then forget him, larger doll
Who would hardly ever loll,
Who would hardly ever smile,
Or bring dill pickles, or core
Fruit, or put salve on a sore.

Leaves his mistress to dismiss
Memories of his kick and kiss,
Grant her lips another smear,
Adjust the posies at her ear,
Quaff an extra pint of beer,
Cross her legs upon the stool,
Slit her eyes and find her fool.

Leaves his devotee to bear
Weight of passing by his chair
And his tavern. Telephone
Hoists her stomach to the air.
Who is starch or who is stone

Washes coffee-cups and hair,
Sweeps, determines what to wear.

In the indignant dark there ride
Roughnesses and spiny things
On infallible hundred heels.
And a bodiless bee stings.
Cyclone concentration reels.
Harried sods dilate, divide,
Suck her sorrowfully inside.

Think of tweaked and twenty-four.
Fuchsias gone or gripped or gray,
All hay-colored that was green.
Soft aesthetic looted, lean.
Crouching low, behind a screen,
Pock-marked eye-light, and the sore
Eaglets of old pride and prey.

Think of almost thoroughly
Derelict and dim and done.
Stroking swallows from the sweat.
Fingering faint violet.
Hugging old and Sunday sun.
Kissing in her kitchenette
The minuets of memory.

Appendix to the Anniad
leaves from a loose-leaf war diary

1

("thousands—killed in action")

You need the untranslatable ice to watch.
You need to loiter a little among the vague
Hushes, the clever evasions of the vagueness
Above the healthy energy of decay.
You need the untranslatable ice to watch,
The purple and black to smell.

Before your horror can be sweet.
Or proper.
Before your grief is other than discreet.

The intellectual damn
Will nurse your half-hurt. Quickly you are well.

But weary. How you yawn, have yet to see
Why nothing exhausts you like this sympathy.

2

The Certainty we two shall meet by God
In a wide Parlor, underneath a Light
Of lights, come Sometime, is no ointment now.
Because we two are worshipers of life,
Being young, being masters of the long-legged stride,
Gypsy arm-swing. We never did learn how
To find white in the Bible. We want nights
Of vague adventure, lips lax wet and warm,
Bees in the stomach, sweat across the brow. Now.

3

the sonnet-ballad

Oh mother, mother, where is happiness?
They took my lover's tallness off to war.
Left me lamenting. Now I cannot guess
What I can use an empty heart-cup for.
He won't be coming back here any more.
Some day the war will end, but, oh, I knew
When he went walking grandly out that door
That my sweet love would have to be untrue.
Would have to be untrue. Would have to court
Coquettish death, whose impudent and strange
Possessive arms and beauty (of a sort)
Can make a hard man hesitate—and change.
And he will be the one to stammer, "Yes."
Oh mother, mother, where is happiness?

The Womanhood

the children of the poor

1

People who have no children can be hard:
Attain a mail of ice and insolence:
Need not pause in the fire, and in no sense
Hesitate in the hurricane to guard.
And when wide world is bitten and bewarred
They perish purely, waving their spirits hence
Without a trace of grace or of offense
To laugh or fail, diffident, wonder-starred.
While through a throttling dark we others hear
The little lifting helplessness, the queer
Whimper-whine; whose unridiculous
Lost softness softly makes a trap for us.
And makes a curse. And makes a sugar of
The malocclusions, the inconditions of love.

2

What shall I give my children? who are poor,
Who are adjudged the leastwise of the land,
Who are my sweetest lepers, who demand
No velvet and no velvety velour;
But who have begged me for a brisk contour,
Crying that they are quasi, contraband
Because unfinished, graven by a hand
Less than angelic, admirable or sure.
My hand is stuffed with mode, design, device.
But I lack access to my proper stone.
And plenitude of plan shall not suffice
Nor grief nor love shall be enough alone
To ratify my little halves who bear
Across an autumn freezing everywhere.

3

And shall I prime my children, pray, to pray?
Mites, come invade most frugal vestibules
Spectered with crusts of penitents' renewals
And all hysterics arrogant for a day.
Instruct yourselves here is no devil to pay.
Children, confine your lights in jellied rules;
Resemble graves; be metaphysical mules;
Learn Lord will not distort nor leave the fray.
Behind the scurryings of your neat motif
I shall wait, if you wish: revise the psalm
If that should frighten you: sew up belief

If that should tear: turn, singularly calm
At forehead and at fingers rather wise,
Holding the bandage ready for your eyes.

4

First fight. Then fiddle. Ply the slipping string
With feathery sorcery; muzzle the note
With hurting love; the music that they wrote
Bewitch, bewilder. Qualify to sing
Threadwise. Devise no salt, no hempen thing
For the dear instrument to bear. Devote
The bow to silks and honey. Be remote
A while from malice and from murdering.
But first to arms, to armor. Carry hate
In front of you and harmony behind.
Be deaf to music and to beauty blind.
Win war. Rise bloody, maybe not too late
For having first to civilize a space
Wherein to play your violin with grace.

5

When my dears die, the festival-colored brightness
That is their motion and mild repartee
Enchanted, a macabre mockery
Charming the rainbow radiance into tightness
And into a remarkable politeness
That is not kind and does not want to be,
May not they in the crisp encounter see

Something to recognize and read as rightness?
I say they may, so granitely discreet,
The little crooked questionings inbound,
Concede themselves on most familiar ground,
Cold an old predicament of the breath:
Adroit, the shapely prefaces complete,
Accept the university of death.

II

Life for my child is simple, and is good.
He knows his wish. Yes, but that is not all.
Because I know mine too.
And we both want joy of undeep and unabiding things,
Like kicking over a chair or throwing blocks out of a window
Or tipping over an icebox pan
Or snatching down curtains or fingering an electric outlet
Or a journey or a friend or an illegal kiss.
No. There is more to it than that.
It is that he has never been afraid.
Rather, he reaches out and lo the chair falls with a beautiful
        crash,
And the blocks fall, down on the people's heads,
And the water comes slooshing sloppily out across the floor.
And so forth.
Not that success, for him, is sure, infallible.
But never has he been afraid to reach.
His lesions are legion.
But reaching is his rule.

the ballad of the light-eyed little girl

Sweet Sally took a cardboard box,
And in went pigeon poor.
Whom she had starved to death but not
For lack of love, be sure.

The wind it harped as twenty men.
The wind it harped like hate.
It whipped our light-eyed little girl,
It made her wince and wait.

It screeched a hundred elegies
As it punished her light eyes
(Though only kindness covered these)
And it made her eyebrows rise.

"Now bury your bird," the wind it bawled,
"And bury him down and down
Who had to put his trust in one
So light-eyed and so brown.

"So light-eyed and so villainous,
Who whooped and who could hum
But could not find the time to toss
Confederate his crumb."

She has taken her passive pigeon poor,
She has buried him down and down.

He never shall sally to Sally
Nor soil any roofs of the town.

She has sprinkled nail polish on dead dandelions.
And children have gathered around
Funeral for him whose epitaph
Is "Pigeon—Under the ground."

IV

A light and diplomatic bird
Is lenient in my window tree.
A quick dilemma of the leaves
Discloses twist and tact to me.

Who strangles his extremest need
For pity of my imminence
On utmost ache and lacquered cold
Is prosperous in proper sense:

He can abash his barmecides;
The fantoccini of his range
Pass over. Vast and secular
And apt and admirably strange.

Augmented by incorrigible
Conviction of his symmetry,
He can afford his sine die.
He can afford to pity me

Whose hours at best are wheats or beiges
Lashed with riot-red and black.
Tabasco at the lapping wave.
Search-light in the secret crack.

Oh open, apostolic height!
And tell my humbug how to start
Bird balance, bleach: make miniature
Valhalla of my heart.

VI

the rites for Cousin Vit

Carried her unprotesting out the door.
Kicked back the casket-stand. But it can't hold her,
That stuff and satin aiming to enfold her,
The lid's contrition nor the bolts before.
Oh oh. Too much. Too much. Even now, surmise,
She rises in the sunshine. There she goes,
Back to the bars she knew and the repose
In love-rooms and the things in people's eyes.
Too vital and too squeaking. Must emerge.
Even now she does the snake-hips with a hiss,
Slops the bad wine across her shantung, talks
Of pregnancy, guitars and bridgework, walks
In parks or alleys, comes haply on the verge
Of happiness, haply hysterics. Is.

VII

I love those little booths at Benvenuti's

They get to Benvenuti's. There are booths
To hide in while observing tropical truths
About this—dusky folk, so clamorous!
So colorfully incorrect,
So amorous,
So flatly brave!
Boothed-in, one can detect,
Dissect.

One knows and scarcely knows what to expect.

What antics, knives, what lurching dirt; what ditty—
Dirty, rich, carmine, hot, not bottled up,
Straining in sexual soprano, cut
And praying in the bass, partial, unpretty.

They sit, sup,
(Whose friends, if not themselves, arrange
To rent in Venice "a very large cabana,
Small palace," and eat mostly what is strange.)
They sit, they settle; presently are met
By the light heat, the lazy upward whine
And lazy croaky downward drawl of "Tanya."
And their interiors sweat.
They lean back in the half-light, stab their stares
At: walls, panels of imitation oak
With would-be marbly look; linoleum squares

Of dusty rose and brown with little white splashes,
White curls; a vendor tidily encased;
Young yellow waiter moving with straight haste,
Old oaken waiter, lolling and amused;
Some paper napkins in a water glass;
Table, initialed, rubbed, as a desk in school.

They stare. They tire. They feel refused,
Feel overwhelmed by subtle treasons!
Nobody here will take the part of jester.

The absolute stutters, and the rationale
Stoops off in astonishment.
But not gaily
And not with their consent.

They play "They All Say I'm The Biggest Fool"
And "Voo Me On The Vot Nay" and "New Lester
Leaps In" and "For Sentimental Reasons."

But how shall they tell people they have been
Out Bronzeville way? For all the nickels in
Have not bought savagery or defined a "folk."

The colored people will not "clown."

The colored people arrive, sit firmly down,
Eat their Express Spaghetti, their T-bone steak,
Handling their steel and crockery with no clatter,
Laugh punily, rise, go firmly out of the door.

VIII

Beverly Hills, Chicago

> "and the people live till they have white hair"
> —E. M. Price

The dry brown coughing beneath their feet,
(Only a while, for the handyman is on his way)
These people walk their golden gardens.
We say ourselves fortunate to be driving by today.

That we may look at them, in their gardens where
The summer ripeness rots. But not raggedly.
Even the leaves fall down in lovelier patterns here.
And the refuse, the refuse is a neat brilliancy.

When they flow sweetly into their houses
With softness and slowness touched by that everlasting gold,
We know what they go to. To tea. But that does not mean
They will throw some little black dots into some water and add
      sugar and the juice of the cheapest lemons that are sold,

While downstairs that woman's vague phonograph bleats,
      "Knock me a kiss."
And the living all to be made again in the sweatingest physical
      manner
Tomorrow. . . . Not that anybody is saying that these people
      have no trouble.
Merely that it is trouble with a gold-flecked beautiful banner.

Nobody is saying that these people do not ultimately cease to
            be. And
Sometimes their passings are even more painful than ours.
It is just that so often they live till their hair is white.
They make excellent corpses, among the expensive flowers. . . .

Nobody is furious. Nobody hates these people.
At least, nobody driving by in this car.
It is only natural, however, that it should occur to us
How much more fortunate they are than we are.

It is only natural that we should look and look
At their wood and brick and stone
And think, while a breath of pine blows,
How different these are from our own.

We do not want them to have less.
But it is only natural that we should think we have not enough.
We drive on, we drive on.
When we speak to each other our voices are a little gruff.

IX

truth

And if sun comes
How shall we greet him?
Shall we not dread him,
Shall we not fear him
After so lengthy a
Session with shade?

Though we have wept for him,
Though we have prayed
All through the night-years—
What if we wake one shimmering morning to
Hear the fierce hammering
Of his firm knuckles
Hard on the door?

Shall we not shudder?—
Shall we not flee
Into the shelter, the dear thick shelter
Of the familiar
Propitious haze?

Sweet is it, sweet is it
To sleep in the coolness
Of snug unawareness.

The dark hangs heavily
Over the eyes.

XI

One wants a Teller in a time like this.

One's not a man, one's not a woman grown.
To bear enormous business all alone.

One cannot walk this winding street with pride,
Straight-shouldered, tranquil-eyed,
Knowing one knows for sure the way back home.
One wonders if one has a home.

One is not certain if or why or how.
One wants a Teller now:—

Put on your rubbers and you won't catch cold.
Here's hell, there's heaven. Go to Sunday School.
Be patient, time brings all good things—(and cool
Strong balm to calm the burning at the brain?)—
Behold, Love's true, and triumphs, and God's actual.

XIV

People protest in sprawling lightless ways
Against their deceivers, they are never meek—
Conceive their furies, and abort them early;
Are hurt, and shout, weep without form, are surly;
Or laugh, but save their censures and their damns.

And ever complex, ever taut, intense,
You hear man crying up to Any one—
"Be my reviver; be my influence,
My reinstated stimulus, my loyal.
Enable me to give my golds goldly,
To win.
To
Take out a skulk, to put a fortitude in.
Give me my life again, whose right is quite
The charm of porcelain, the vigor of stone."

And he will follow many a cloven foot.

XV

Men of careful turns, haters of forks in the road,
The strain at the eye, that puzzlement, that awe—
Grant me that I am human, that I hurt,
That I can cry.

Not that I now ask alms, in shame gone hollow,
Nor cringe outside the loud and sumptuous gate.
Admit me to our mutual estate.

Open my rooms, let in the light and air.
Reserve my service at the human feast.
And let the joy continue. Do not hoard silence
For the moment when I enter, tardily,
To enjoy my height among you. And to love you
No more as a woman loves a drunken mate,
Restraining full caress and good My Dear,
Even pity for the heaviness and the need—
Fearing sudden fire out of the uncaring mouth,
Boiling in the slack eyes, and the traditional blow.
Next, the indifference formal, deep and slow.

Comes in your graceful glider and benign,
To smile upon me bigly; now desires
Me easy, easy; claims the days are softer
Than they were; murmurs reflectively "Remember
When cruelty, metal, public, uncomplex,
Trampled you obviously and every hour. . . ."
(Now cruelty flaunts diplomas, is elite,
Delicate, has polish, knows how to be discreet):
　　　　　Requests my patience, wills me to be calm,

Brings me a chair, but the one with broken straw,
Whispers "My friend, no thing is without flaw.
If prejudice is native—and it is—you
Will find it ineradicable—not to
Be juggled, not to be altered at all,
But left unvexed at its place in the properness
Of things, even to be given (with grudging)
    honor.

        What
We are to hope is that intelligence
Can sugar up our prejudice with politeness.
Politeness will take care of what needs caring.
For the line is there.
And has a meaning. So our fathers said—
And they were wise—we think—At any rate,
They were older than ourselves. And the report is
What's old is wise. At any rate, the line is
Long and electric. Lean beyond and nod.
Be sprightly. Wave. Extend your hand and teeth.
But never forget it stretches there beneath."

The toys are all grotesque
And not for lovely hands; are dangerous,
Serrate in open and artful places. Rise.
Let us combine. There are no magics or elves
Or timely godmothers to guide us. We are lost, must
Wizard a track through our own screaming weed.

THE BEAN EATERS

In Honor of David Anderson Brooks,
My Father

July 30, 1883–November 21, 1959

A dryness is upon the house
My father loved and tended.
Beyond his firm and sculptured door
His light and lease have ended.

He walks the valleys, now—replies
To sun and wind forever.
No more the cramping chamber's chill,
No more the hindering fever.

Now out upon the wide clean air
My father's soul revives,
All innocent of self-interest
And the fear that strikes and strives.

He who was Goodness, Gentleness,
And Dignity is free,
Translates to public Love
Old private charity.

My Little 'Bout-Town Gal

Roger of Rhodes

My little 'bout-town gal has gone
'Bout town with powder and blue dye
On her pale lids and on her lips
Dye sits quite carminely.

I'm scarcely healthy-hearted or human.
What can I teach my cheated Woman?

My Tondeleyo, my black blonde
Will not be homing soon.
None shall secure her save the late the
Detective fingers of the moon.

Strong Men, Riding Horses

Lester after the Western

Strong Men, riding horses. In the West
On a range five hundred miles. A Thousand. Reaching
From dawn to sunset. Rested blue to orange.
From hope to crying. Except that Strong Men are
Desert-eyed. Except that Strong Men are
Pasted to stars already. Have their cars
Beneath them. Rentless, too. Too broad of chest
To shrink when the Rough Man hails. Too flailing
To redirect the Challenger, when the challenge
Nicks; slams; buttonholes. Too saddled.

I am not like that. I pay rent, am addled
By illegible landlords, run, if robbers call.

What mannerisms I present, employ,
Are camouflage, and what my mouths remark
To word-wall off that broadness of the dark
Is pitiful.
I am not brave at all.

The Bean Eaters

They eat beans mostly, this old yellow pair.
Dinner is a casual affair.
Plain chipware on a plain and creaking wood,
Tin flatware.

Two who are Mostly Good.
Two who have lived their day,
But keep on putting on their clothes
And putting things away.

And remembering . . .
Remembering, with twinklings and twinges,
As they lean over the beans in their rented back room that is full
      of beads and receipts and dolls and cloths, tobacco
      crumbs, vases and fringes.

We Real Cool

**The Pool Players.
Seven at the Golden Shovel.**

We real cool. We
Left school. We

Lurk late. We
Strike straight. We

Sing sin. We
Thin gin. We

Jazz June. We
Die soon.

Old Mary

My last defense
Is the present tense.

It little hurts me now to know
I shall not go

Cathedral-hunting in Spain
Nor cherrying in Michigan or Maine.

A Bronzeville Mother Loiters in Mississippi.
Meanwhile, a Mississippi Mother Burns Bacon.

From the first it had been like a
Ballad. It had the beat inevitable. It had the blood.
A wildness cut up, and tied in little bunches,
Like the four-line stanzas of the ballads she had never quite
Understood—the ballads they had set her to, in school.

Herself: the milk-white maid, the "maid mild"
Of the ballad. Pursued
By the Dark Villain. Rescued by the Fine Prince.
The Happiness-Ever-After.
That was worth anything.
It was good to be a "maid mild."
That made the breath go fast.

Her bacon burned. She
Hastened to hide it in the step-on can, and
Drew more strips from the meat case. The eggs and sour-milk
        biscuits
Did well. She set out a jar
Of her new quince preserve.

. . . But there was a something about the matter of the Dark
          Villain.
He should have been older, perhaps.
The hacking down of a villain was more fun to think about
When his menace possessed undisputed breadth, undisputed
          height,
And a harsh kind of vice.
And best of all, when his history was cluttered
With the bones of many eaten knights and princesses.

The fun was disturbed, then all but nullified
When the Dark Villain was a blackish child
Of fourteen, with eyes still too young to be dirty,
And a mouth too young to have lost every reminder
Of its infant softness.

That boy must have been surprised! For
These were grown-ups. Grown-ups were supposed to be wise.
And the Fine Prince—and that other—so tall, so broad, so
Grown! Perhaps the boy had never guessed
That the trouble with grown-ups was that under the
          magnificent shell of adulthood, just under,
Waited the baby full of tantrums.
It occurred to her that there may have been something
Ridiculous in the picture of the Fine Prince
Rushing (rich with the breadth and height and
Mature solidness whose lack, in the Dark Villain, was impressing
          her,
Confronting her more and more as this first day after the trial

And acquittal wore on) rushing
With his heavy companion to hack down (unhorsed)
That little foe.
So much had happened, she could not remember now what
        that foe had done
Against her, or if anything had been done.
The one thing in the world that she did know and knew
With terrifying clarity was that her composition
Had disintegrated. That, although the pattern prevailed,
The breaks were everywhere. That she could think
Of no thread capable of the necessary
Sew-work.

She made the babies sit in their places at the table.
Then, before calling Him, she hurried
To the mirror with her comb and lipstick. It was necessary
To be more beautiful than ever.
The beautiful wife.
For sometimes she fancied he looked at her as though
Measuring her. As if he considered, Had she been worth It?
Had *she* been worth the blood, the cramped cries, the little
        stuttering bravado,
The gradual dulling of those Negro eyes,
The sudden, overwhelming *little-boyness* in that barn?
Whatever she might feel or half-feel, the lipstick necessity was
        something apart. He must never conclude
That she had not been worth It.

He sat down, the Fine Prince, and
Began buttering a biscuit. He looked at his hands.

He twisted in his chair, he scratched his nose.
He glanced again, almost secretly, at his hands.
More papers were in from the North, he mumbled. More
    meddling headlines.
With their pepper-words, "bestiality," and "barbarism," and
"Shocking."
The half-sneers he had mastered for the trial worked across
His sweet and pretty face.

What he'd like to do, he explained, was kill them all.
The time lost. The unwanted fame.
Still, it had been fun to show those intruders
A thing or two. To show that snappy-eyed mother,
That sassy, Northern, brown-black—

Nothing could stop Mississippi.
He knew that. Big Fella
Knew that.
And, what was so good, Mississippi knew that.
Nothing and nothing could stop Mississippi.
They could send in their petitions, and scar
Their newspapers with bleeding headlines. Their governors
Could appeal to Washington . . .

"What I want," the older baby said, "is 'lasses on my jam."
Whereupon the younger baby
Picked up the molasses pitcher and threw
The molasses in his brother's face. Instantly
The Fine Prince leaned across the table and slapped
The small and smiling criminal.

She did not speak. When the Hand
Came down and away, and she could look at her child,
At her baby-child,
She could think only of blood.
Surely her baby's cheek
Had disappeared, and in its place, surely,
Hung a heaviness, a lengthening red, a red that had no end.
She shook her head. It was not true, of course.
It was not true at all. The
Child's face was as always, the
Color of the paste in her paste-jar.

She left the table, to the tune of the children's lamentations,
        which were shriller
Than ever. She
Looked out of a window. She said not a word. *That*
Was one of the new Somethings—
The fear,
Tying her as with iron.

Suddenly she felt his hands upon her. He had followed her
To the window. The children were whimpering now.
Such bits of tots. And she, their mother,
Could not protect them. She looked at her shoulders, still
Gripped in the claim of his hands. She tried, but could not resist
        the idea
That a red ooze was seeping, spreading darkly, thickly, slowly,
Over her white shoulders, her own shoulders,
And over all of Earth and Mars.

He whispered something to her, did the Fine Prince, something
About love, something about love and night and intention.

She heard no hoof-beat of the horse and saw no flash of the
    shining steel.

He pulled her face around to meet
His, and there it was, close close,
For the first time in all those days and nights.
His mouth, wet and red,
So very, very, very red,
Closed over hers.

Then a sickness heaved within her. The courtroom Coca-Cola,
The courtroom beer and hate and sweat and drone,
Pushed like a wall against her. She wanted to bear it.
But his mouth would not go away and neither would the
Decapitated exclamation points in that Other Woman's eyes.

She did not scream.
She stood there.
But a hatred for him burst into glorious flower,
And its perfume enclasped them—big,
Bigger than all magnolias.

The last bleak news of the ballad.
The rest of the rugged music.
The last quatrain.

The Last Quatrain of the Ballad of Emmett Till

after the murder,
after the burial

Emmett's mother is a pretty-faced thing;
                the tint of pulled taffy.
She sits in a red room,
                drinking black coffee.
She kisses her killed boy.
                And she is sorry.
Chaos in windy grays
                through a red prairie.

Mrs. Small

Mrs. Small went to the kitchen for her pocketbook
And came back to the living room with a peculiar look
And the coffee pot.
Pocketbook. Pot.
Pot. Pocketbook.

The insurance man was waiting there
With superb and cared-for hair.
His face did not have much time.
He did not glance with sublime
Love upon the little plump tan woman
With the half-open mouth and the half-mad eyes
And the smile half-human
Who stood in the middle of the living-room floor planning
    apple pies
And graciously offering him a steaming coffee pot.
Pocketbook. Pot.

"Oh!" Mrs. Small came to her senses,
Peered earnestly through thick lenses,
Jumped terribly. This, too, was a mistake,

Unforgivable no matter how much she had to bake.
For there can be no whiter whiteness than this one:
An insurance man's shirt on its morning run.
This Mrs. Small now soiled
With a pair of brown
Spurts (just recently boiled)
Of the "very best coffee in town."

"The best coffee in town is what *you* make, Delphine! There is
        none dandier!"
Those were the words of the pleased Jim Small—
Who was no bandier of words at all.
Jim Small was likely to give you a good swat
When he was *not*
Pleased. He was, absolutely, no bandier.

"I don't know where my mind is this morning,"
Said Mrs. Small, scorning
Apologies! For there was so much
For which to apologize! Oh such
Mountains of things, she'd never get anything done
If she begged forgiveness for each one.

She paid him.

But apologies and her hurry would not mix.
The six
Daughters were a-yell, a-scramble, in the hall. The four
Sons (horrors) could not be heard any more.

No.
The insurance man would have to glare
Idiotically into her own sterile stare
A moment—then depart,
Leaving her to release her heart
And dizziness

And silence her six
And mix
Her spices and core
And slice her apples, and find her four.
Continuing her part
Of the world's business.

Jessie Mitchell's Mother

Into her mother's bedroom to wash the ballooning body.
"My mother is jelly-hearted and she has a brain of jelly:
Sweet, quiver-soft, irrelevant. Not essential.
Only a habit would cry if she should die.
A pleasant sort of fool without the least iron. . . .
Are you better, mother, do you think it will come today?"
The stretched yellow rag that was Jessie Mitchell's mother
Reviewed her. Young, and so thin, and so straight.
So straight! as if nothing could ever bend her.
But poor men would bend her, and doing things with poor
      men,
Being much in bed, and babies would bend her over,
And the rest of things in life that were for poor women,
Coming to them grinning and pretty with intent to bend and to
      kill.
Comparisons shattered her heart, ate at her bulwarks:
The shabby and the bright: she, almost hating her daughter,
Crept into an old sly refuge: "Jessie's black
And her way will be black, and jerkier even than mine.
Mine, in fact, because I was lovely, had flowers
Tucked in the jerks, flowers were here and there. . . ."
She revived for the moment settled and dried-up triumphs,

Forced perfume into old petals, pulled up the droop,
Refueled
Triumphant long-exhaled breaths.
Her exquisite yellow youth . . .

The Chicago Defender Sends a Man to Little Rock

Fall, 1957

In Little Rock the people bear
Babes, and comb and part their hair
And watch the want ads, put repair
To roof and latch. While wheat toast burns
A woman waters multiferns.

Time upholds or overturns
The many, tight, and small concerns.

In Little Rock the people sing
Sunday hymns like anything,
Through Sunday pomp and polishing.

And after testament and tunes,
Some soften Sunday afternoons
With lemon tea and Lorna Doones.

I forecast
And I believe

Come Christmas Little Rock will cleave
To Christmas tree and trifle, weave,
From laugh and tinsel, texture fast.

In Little Rock is baseball; Barcarolle.
That hotness in July . . . the uniformed figures raw and
      implacable
And not intellectual,
Batting the hotness or clawing the suffering dust.
The Open Air Concert, on the special twilight green. . . .
When Beethoven is brutal or whispers to lady-like air.
Blanket-sitters are solemn, as Johann troubles to lean
To tell them what to mean. . . .

There is love, too, in Little Rock. Soft women softly
Opening themselves in kindness,
Or, pitying one's blindness,
Awaiting one's pleasure
In azure
Glory with anguished rose at the root. . . .
To wash away old semi-discomfitures.
They re-teach purple and unsullen blue.
The wispy soils go. And uncertain
Half-havings have they clarified to sures.

In Little Rock they know
Not answering the telephone is a way of rejecting life,
That it is our business to be bothered, is our business
To cherish bores or boredom, be polite
To lies and love and many-faceted fuzziness.

I scratch my head, massage the hate-I-had.
I blink across my prim and pencilled pad.
The saga I was sent for is not down.
Because there is a puzzle in this town.
The biggest News I do not dare
Telegraph to the Editor's chair:
"They are like people everywhere."

The angry Editor would reply
In hundred harryings of Why.

And true, they are hurling spittle, rock,
Garbage and fruit in Little Rock.
And I saw coiling storm a-writhe
On bright madonnas. And a scythe
Of men harassing brownish girls.
(The bows and barrettes in the curls
And braids declined away from joy.)

I saw a bleeding brownish boy. . . .

The lariat lynch-wish I deplored.

The loveliest lynchee was our Lord.

The Lovers of the Poor

arrive. The Ladies from the Ladies'
       Betterment League
Arrive in the afternoon, the late light slanting
In diluted gold bars across the boulevard brag
Of proud, seamed faces with mercy and murder hinting
Here, there, interrupting, all deep and debonair,
The pink paint on the innocence of fear;
Walk in a gingerly manner up the hall.
Cutting with knives served by their softest care,
Served by their love, so barbarously fair.
Whose mothers taught: You'd better not be cruel!
You had better not throw stones upon the wrens!
Herein they kiss and coddle and assault
Anew and dearly in the innocence
With which they baffle nature. Who are full,
Sleek, tender-clad, fit, fiftyish, a-glow, all
Sweetly abortive, hinting at fat fruit,
Judge it high time that fiftyish fingers felt
Beneath the lovelier planes of enterprise.
To resurrect. To moisten with milky chill.

To be a random hitching-post or plush.
To be, for wet eyes, random and handy hem.
                    Their guild is giving money to the poor.
The worthy poor. The very very worthy
And beautiful poor. Perhaps just not too swarthy?
Perhaps just not too dirty nor too dim
Nor—passionate. In truth, what they could wish
Is—something less than derelict or dull.
Not staunch enough to stab, though, gaze for gaze!
God shield them sharply from the beggar-bold!
The noxious needy ones whose battle's bald
Nonetheless for being voiceless, hits one down.
                    But it's all so bad! and entirely too much for
                    them.
The stench; the urine, cabbage, and dead beans,
Dead porridges of assorted dusty grains,
The old smoke, *heavy* diapers, and, they're told,
Something called chitterlings. The darkness. Drawn
Darkness, or dirty light. The soil that stirs.
The soil that looks the soil of centuries.
And for that matter the *general* oldness. Old
Wood. Old marble. Old tile. Old old old.
Not homekind Oldness! Not Lake Forest, Glencoe.
Nothing is sturdy, nothing is majestic,
There is no quiet drama, no rubbed glaze, no
Unkillable infirmity of such
A tasteful turn as lately they have left,
Glencoe, Lake Forest, and to which their cars
Must presently restore them. When they're done
With dullards and distortions of this fistic

Patience of the poor and put-upon.

                They've never seen such a make-do-ness as
Newspaper rugs before! In this, this "flat,"
Their hostess is gathering up the oozed, the rich
Rugs of the morning (tattered! the bespattered. . . .)
Readies to spread clean rugs for afternoon.
Here is a scene for you. The Ladies look,
In horror, behind a substantial citizeness
Whose trains clank out across her swollen heart.
Who, arms akimbo, almost fills a door.
All tumbling children, quilts dragged to the floor
And tortured thereover, potato peelings, soft-
Eyed kitten, hunched-up, haggard, to-be-hurt.

            Their League is allotting largesse to the Lost.
But to put their clean, their pretty money, to put
Their money collected from delicate rose-fingers
Tipped with their hundred flawless rose-nails seems . . .

            They own Spode, Lowestoft, candelabra,
Mantels, and hostess gowns, and sunburst clocks,
Turtle soup, Chippendale, red satin "hangings,"
Aubussons and Hattie Carnegie. They Winter
In Palm Beach; cross the Water in June; attend,
When suitable, the nice Art Institute;
Buy the right books in the best bindings; saunter
On Michigan, Easter mornings, in sun or wind.
Oh Squalor! This sick four-story hulk, this fibre
With fissures everywhere! Why, what are bringings
Of loathe-love largesse? What shall peril hungers
So old old, what shall flatter the desolate?
Tin can, blocked fire escape and chitterling

And swaggering seeking youth and the puzzled wreckage
Of the middle passage, and urine and stale shames
And, again, the porridges of the underslung
And children children children. Heavens! That
Was a rat, surely, off there, in the shadows? Long
And long-tailed? Gray? The Ladies from the Ladies'
Betterment League agree it will be better
To achieve the outer air that rights and steadies,
To hie to a house that does not holler, to ring
Bells elsetime, better presently to cater
To no more Possibilities, to get
Away. Perhaps the money can be posted.
Perhaps they two may choose another Slum!
Some serious sooty half-unhappy home!—
Where loathe-love likelier may be invested.

                      Keeping their scented bodies in the center
Of the hall as they walk down the hysterical hall,
They allow their lovely skirts to graze no wall,
Are off at what they manage of a canter,
And, resuming all the clues of what they were,
Try to avoid inhaling the laden air.

A Sunset of the City

Kathleen Eileen

Already I am no longer looked at with lechery or love.
My daughters and sons have put me away with marbles and
       dolls,
Are gone from the house.
My husband and lovers are pleasant or somewhat polite
And night is night.

It is a real chill out,
The genuine thing.
I am not deceived, I do not think it is still summer
Because sun stays and birds continue to sing.

It is summer gone that I see, it is summer-gone.
The sweet flowers indrying and dying down,
The grasses forgetting their blaze and consenting to brown.

It is a real chill out. The fall crisp comes.
I am aware there is winter to heed.
There is no warm house
That is fitted with my need.

I am cold in this cold house this house
Whose washed echoes are tremulous down lost halls.
I am a woman, and dusty, standing among new affairs.
I am a woman who hurries through her prayers.

Tin intimations of a quiet core to be my
Desert and my dear relief
Come: there shall be such islanding from grief,
And small communion with the master shore.
Twang they. And I incline this ear to tin,
Consult a dual dilemma. Whether to dry
In humming pallor or to leap and die.

Somebody muffed it? Somebody wanted to joke.

A Man of the Middle Class

I'm what has gone out blithely and with noise
Returning! I'm what rushed around to pare
Down rind, to find fruit frozen under there.

I am bedraggled, with sundry dusts to be shed;
Trailing desperate tarnished tassels. These strident Aprils
With terrifying polkas and Bugle Calls
Confound me.

—Although I've risen! and my back is bold.
My tongue is brainy, choosing from among
Care, rage, surprise, despair, and choosing care.
I'm semi-splendid within what I've defended.

Yet, there I totter, there limp laxly. My
Uncomely trudge
To Plateau That and platitudinous Plateau
Whichever is no darling to my grudge-
Choked industry or usual alcohol.

I've roses to guard
In the architectural prettiness of my yard.

(But there are no paths remarkable for wide
Believable welcomes.)

I have loved directions.
I have loved orders and an iron to stride, I,
Whose hands are papers now,
Fit only for tossing in this outrageous air.

Not God nor grace nor candy balls
Will get me everything different and the same!

My wife has canvas walls.

My wife never quite forgets to put flowers in vases,
Bizarre prints in the most unusual places,
Give teas for poets, wear odoriferous furs.
An awful blooming is hers.

I've antique firearms. Blackamoors. Chinese
Rugs. Ivories.
Bronzes. Everything I Wanted.
But have I answers? Oh methinks
I've answers such as have
The executives I copied long ago,
The ones who, forfeiting Vicks salve,
Prayer book and Mother, shot themselves last Sunday.
All forsaking
All that was theirs but for their money's taking.

I've answers such as Giants used to know.
There's a Giant who'll jump next Monday; all forsaking
Wives, safes and solitaire
And the elegant statue standing at the foot of the stair.

The Crazy Woman

I shall not sing a May song.
A May song should be gay.
I'll wait until November
And sing a song of gray.

I'll wait until November.
That is the time for me.
I'll go out in the frosty dark
And sing most terribly.

And all the little people
Will stare at me and say,
"That is the Crazy Woman
Who would not sing in May."

Bronzeville Man with a Belt in the Back

In such an armor he may rise and raid
The dark cave after midnight, unafraid,
And slice the shadows with his able sword
Of good broad nonchalance, hashing them down.

And come out and accept the gasping crowd,
Shake off the praises with an airiness.
And, searching, see love shining in an eye,
But never smile.

In such an armor he cannot be slain.

A Lovely Love

Let it be alleys. Let it be a hall
Whose janitor javelins epithet and thought
To cheapen hyacinth darkness that we sought
And played we found, rot, make the petals fall.
Let it be stairways, and a splintery box
Where you have thrown me, scraped me with your kiss,
Have honed me, have released me after this
Cavern kindness, smiled away our shocks.
That is the birthright of our lovely love
In swaddling clothes. Not like that Other one.
Not lit by any fondling star above.
Not found by any wise men, either. Run.
People are coming. They must not catch us here
Definitionless in this strict atmosphere.

A Penitent Considers Another Coming of Mary

For Reverend Theodore Richardson

If Mary came would Mary
Forgive, as Mothers may,
And sad and second Saviour
Furnish us today?

She would not shake her head and leave
This military air,
But ratify a modern hay,
And put her Baby there.

Mary would not punish men—
If Mary came again.

Bronzeville Woman in a Red Hat

hires out to Mrs. Miles

I

They had never had one in the house before.
            The strangeness of it all. Like unleashing
A lion, really. Poised
To pounce. A puma. A panther. A black
Bear.
There it stood in the door,
Under a red hat that was rash, but refreshing—
In a tasteless way, of course—across the dull dare,
The semi-assault of that extraordinary blackness.
The slackness
Of that light pink mouth told little. The eyes told of heavy
            care. . . .
But that was neither here nor there,
And nothing to a wage-paying mistress as should
Be getting her due whether life had been good
For her slave, or bad.
There it stood

In the door. They had never had
One in the house before.

But the Irishwoman had left!
A message had come.
Something about a murder at home.
A daughter's husband—"berserk," that was the phrase:
The dear man had "gone berserk"
And short work—
With a hammer—had been made
Of this daughter and her nights and days.
The Irishwoman (underpaid,
Mrs. Miles remembered with smiles),
Who was a perfect jewel, a red-faced trump,
A good old sort, a baker
Of rum cake, a maker
Of Mustard, would never return.
Mrs. Miles had begged the bewitched woman
To finish, at least, the biscuit blending,
To tarry till the curry was done,
To show some concern
For the burning soup, to attend to the tending
Of the tossed salad. "Inhuman,"
Patsy Houlihan had called Mrs. Miles.
"Inhuman." And "a fool."
And "a cool
One."

The Alert Agency had leafed through its files—
On short notice could offer

Only this dusky duffer
That now made its way to her kitchen and sat on her kitchen
        stool.

II

Her creamy child kissed by the black maid! square on the
        mouth!
World yelled, world writhed, world turned to light and rolled
Into her kitchen, nearly knocked her down.

Quotations, of course, from baby books were great
Ready armor; (but her animal distress
Wore, too and under, a subtler metal dress,
Inheritance of approximately hate.)
Say baby shrieked to see his finger bleed,
Wished human humoring—there was a kind
Of unintimate love, a love more of the mind
To order the nebulousness of that need.
—This was the way to put it, this the relief.
This sprayed a honey upon marvelous grime.
This told it possible to postpone the reef.
Fashioned a huggable darling out of crime.
Made monster personable in personal sight
By cracking mirrors down the personal night.

Disgust crawled through her as she chased the theme.
She, quite supposing purity despoiled,
Committed to sourness, disordered, soiled,

Went in to pry the ordure from the cream.
Cooing, "Come." (Come out of the cannibal wilderness,
Dirt, dark, into the sun and bloomful air.
Return to freshness of your right world, wear
Sweetness again. Be done with beast, duress.)

Child with continuing cling issued his No in final fire,
  Kissed back the colored maid,
  Not wise enough to freeze or be afraid.
  Conscious of kindness, easy creature bond.
  Love had been handy and rapid to respond.

Heat at the hairline, heat between the bowels,
Examining seeming coarse unnatural scene,
She saw all things except herself serene:
Child, big black woman, pretty kitchen towels.

In Emanuel's Nightmare: Another Coming of Christ

**(Speaks, among spirit questioners,
of marvelous spirit affairs.)**

There had been quiet all that afternoon.
Just such a quiet afternoon as any,
Though with a brighter and a freer air.
The sleepy sun sat on us, and those clouds
Dragged dreamily. Well, it was interesting—
How silence could give place to such a noise.
But now—is noise the word? Is that exact?
I think not.

I'll try to name it. Naming is my line.
I won the Great War-Naming Contest. Ah,
I put it over on them all. I beat
Them all. I wear an honor on my name—
Sound wasn't in it. Though it was loud enough.
I'd say it was a heat.

But it took us. Did with us as it would.
Wound us in balls, unraveled, wound again.

And women screamed. "The Judgment Day has come."
And little children gathered up the cry.
It was then that they knocked each other down
To get to—Where? But they were used to Doors.
Thought they had but to beat their Fellow Man
To get to and get out of one again.

It wasn't Judgment Day. (For we are here.)
And presently the people knew, and sighed.
Out of that heaven a most beautiful Man
Came down. But now is coming quite the word?
It wasn't coming. I'd say it was—a Birth.
The man was born out of the heaven, in truth.
Yet no parturient creature ever knew
That naturalness, that hurtlessness, that ease.

How He was tall and strong!
How He was cold-browed! How He mildly smiled!
How the voice played on the heavy hope of the air
And loved our hearts out!
Why, it was such a voice as gave me eyes
To see my Fellow Man of all the world,
There with me, listening.

He had come down, He said, to clean the earth
Of the dirtiness of war.

Now tell of why His power failed Him there?
His power did not fail. It was that, simply,
He found how much the people wanted war.

How much it was their creed, and their good joy.
And what they lived for. He had not the heart
To take away their chief sweet delectation.

We tear—as a decent gesture, a tact—we tear
Laxly again at our lax, our tired hair.

The people wanted war. War's in their hearts.
        (In me, in your snag-toothed fool
Who won the Great War-Naming Contest and
All the years since has bragged how he did Beat
His Fellow Man.) It is the human aim.
Without, there would be no hate. No Diplomats.
And households would be fresh and frictionless.

God's Son went home. Among us it is whispered
He cried the tears of men.

Feeling, in fact,
We have no need of peace.

The Ballad of Rudolph Reed

Rudolph Reed was oaken.
His wife was oaken too.
And his two good girls and his good little man
Oakened as they grew.

"I am not hungry for berries.
I am not hungry for bread.
But hungry hungry for a house
Where at night a man in bed

"May never hear the plaster
Stir as if in pain.
May never hear the roaches
Falling like fat rain.

"Where never wife and children need
Go blinking through the gloom.
Where every room of many rooms
Will be full of room.

"Oh my home may have its east or west
Or north or south behind it.

All I know is I shall know it,
And fight for it when I find it."

It was in a street of bitter white
That he made his application.
For Rudolph Reed was oakener
Than others in the nation.

The agent's steep and steady stare
Corroded to a grin.
Why, you black old, tough old hell of a man,
Move your family in!

Nary a grin grinned Rudolph Reed,
Nary a curse cursed he,
But moved in his House. With his dark little wife,
And his dark little children three.

A neighbor would *look,* with a yawning eye
That squeezed into a slit.
But the Rudolph Reeds and the children three
Were too joyous to notice it.

For were they not firm in a home of their own
With windows everywhere
And a beautiful banistered stair
And a front yard for flowers and a back yard for grass?

The first night, a rock, big as two fists.
The second, a rock big as three.

But nary a curse cursed Rudolph Reed.
(Though oaken as man could be.)

The third night, a silvery ring of glass.
Patience ached to endure.
But he looked, and lo! small Mabel's blood
Was staining her gaze so pure.

Then up did rise our Rudolph Reed
And pressed the hand of his wife,
And went to the door with a thirty-four
And a beastly butcher knife.

He ran like a mad thing into the night.
And the words in his mouth were stinking.
By the time he had hurt his first white man
He was no longer thinking.

By the time he had hurt his fourth white man
Rudolph Reed was dead.
His neighbors gathered and kicked his corpse.
"Nigger—" his neighbors said.

Small Mabel whimpered all night long,
For calling herself the cause.
Her oak-eyed mother did no thing
But change the bloody gauze.

NEW POEMS

Riders to the Blood-red Wrath

My proper prudence toward his proper probe
Astonished their ancestral seemliness.
It was a not-nice risk, a wrought risk, was
An indelicate risk, they thought. And an excess.
Howas I handled my discordances
And prides and apoplectic ice, howas
I reined my charger, channeled the fit fume
Of his most splendid honorable jazz
Escaped the closing and averted sight
Waiving all witness except of rotted flowers
Framed in maimed velvet. That mad demi-art
Of ancient and irrevocable hours.
Waiving all witness except of dimnesses
From which extrude beloved and pennant arms
Of a renegade death impatient at his shrine
And keen to share the gases of his charms.
They veer to vintage. Careening from tomorrows.
Blaring away from my just genesis.
They loot Last Night. They hug old graves, root up
Decomposition, warm it with a kiss.

The National Anthem vampires at the blood.
I am a uniform. Not brusque. I bray

Through blur and blunder in a little voice!
This is a tender grandeur, a tied fray!
Under macabres, stratagem and fair
Fine smiles upon the face of holocaust,
My scream! unedited, unfrivolous.
My laboring unlatched braid of heat and frost.
I hurt. I keep that scream in at what pain:
At what repeal of salvage and eclipse.
Army unhonored, meriting the gold, I
Have sewn my guns inside my burning lips.

Did they detect my parleys and replies?
My Revolution pushed his twin the mare,
The she-thing with the soft eyes that conspire
To lull off men, before him everywhere.
Perhaps they could not see what wheedling bent
Her various heart in mottles of submission
And sent her into a firm skirmish which
Has tickled out the enemy's sedition.

They do not see how deftly I endure.
Deep down the whirlwind of good rage I store
Commemorations in an utter thrall.
Although I need not eat them any more.

I remember kings.
A blossoming palace. Silver. Ivory.
The conventional wealth of stalking Africa.
All bright, all Bestial. Snarling marvelously.

I remember my right to roughly run and roar.
My right to raid the sun, consult the moon,
Nod to my princesses or split them open,
To flay my lions, eat blood with a spoon.
You never saw such running and such roaring!—
Nor heard a burgeoning heart so craze and pound!—
Nor sprang to such a happy rape of heaven!
Nor sanctioned such a kinship with the ground!

And I remember blazing dementias
Aboard such trade as maddens any man.
. . . The mate and captain fragrantly reviewed
The fragrant hold and presently began
Their retching rampage among their luminous
Black pudding, among the guttural chained slime:
Half fainting from their love affair with fetors
That pledged a haughty allegiance for all time.

I recollect the latter lease and lash
And labor that defiled the bone, that thinned
My blood and blood-line. All my climate my
Foster designers designed and disciplined.

But my detention and my massive stain,
And my distortion and my Calvary
I grind into a little light lorgnette
Most sly: to read man's inhumanity.
And I remark my Matter is not all.

Man's chopped in China, in India indented.
From Israel what's Arab is resented.
Europe candies custody and war.

Behind my exposé
I formalize my pity: "*I* shall cite,
Star, and esteem all that which is of woman,
Human and hardly human."

Democracy and Christianity
Recommence with me.

And I ride ride I ride on to the end—
Where glowers my continuing Calvary.
I,
My fellows, and those canny consorts of
Our spread hands in this contretemps-for-love
Ride into wrath, wraith and menagerie

To fail, to flourish, to wither or to win.
We lurch, distribute, we extend, begin.

The Empty Woman

The empty woman took toys!
     In her sisters' homes
Were little girls and boys.

The empty woman had hats
To show. With feathers. Wore combs
In polished waves. Wooed cats

And pigeons. Shopped.
Shopped hard for nephew-toys,
Niece-toys. Made taffy. Popped

Popcorn and hated her sisters,
Featherless and waveless but able to
Mend measles, nag noses, blast blisters

And all day waste wordful girls
And war-boys, and all day
Say "Oh God!"—and tire among curls

And plump legs and proud muscle
And blackened school-bags, babushkas, torn socks,
And bouffants that bustle, and rustle.

To Be in Love

To be in love
Is to touch things with a lighter hand.

In yourself you stretch, you are well.

You look at things
Through his eyes.
A Cardinal is red.
A sky is blue.
Suddenly you know he knows too.
He is not there but
You know you are tasting together
The winter, or light spring weather.

His hand to take your hand is overmuch.
Too much to bear.

You cannot look in his eyes
Because your pulse must not say
What must not be said.

When he
Shuts a door—

Is not there—
Your arms are water.

And you are free
With a ghastly freedom.

You are the beautiful half
Of a golden hurt.

You remember and covet his mouth,
To touch, to whisper on.

Oh when to declare
Is certain Death!

Oh when to apprize
Is to mesmerize,

To see fall down, the Column of Gold,
Into the commonest ash.

Of Robert Frost

There is a little lightning in his eyes.
Iron at the mouth.
His brows ride neither too far up nor down.

He is splendid. With a place to stand.

Some glowing in the common blood.
Some specialness within.

Langston Hughes

      is merry glory.
Is saltatory.
Yet grips his right of twisting free.

Has a long reach,
Strong speech,
Remedial fears.
Muscular tears.

Holds horticulture
In the eye of the vulture
Infirm profession.
In the Compression—
In mud and blood and sudden death—
In the breath
Of the holocaust he
Is helmsman, hatchet, headlight.
See
One restless in the exotic time! and ever,
Till the air is cured of its fever.

A Catch of Shy Fish

garbageman: the man with the orderly mind

What do you think of us in fuzzy endeavor, you whose
        directions are sterling, whose lunge is straight?
Can you make a reason, how can you pardon us who memorize
        the rules and never score?
Who memorize the rules from your own text but never quite
        transfer them to the game,
Who never quite receive the whistling ball, who gawk, begin to
        absorb the crowd's own roar.

Is earnestness enough, may earnestness attract or lead to light;
Is light enough, if hands in clumsy frenzy, flimsy whimsicality,
        enlist;
Is light enough when this bewilderment crying against the dark
        shuts down the shades?
    Dilute confusion. Find and explode our mist.

sick man looks at flowers

You are sick and old, and there is a closing in—
The eyes gone dead to all that would beguile.

Echoes are dull and the body accepts no touch
Except its pain. Mind is a little isle.

But now invades this impudence of red!
This ripe rebuke, this burgeoning affluence
Mocks me and mocks the desert of my bed.

old people working (garden, car)

Old people working. Making a gift of garden.
Or washing a car, so some one else may ride.
A note of alliance, an eloquence of pride.
A way of greeting or sally to the world.

weaponed woman

Well, life has been a baffled vehicle
And baffling. But she fights, and
Has fought, according to her lights and
The lenience of her whirling-place.

She fights with semi-folded arms,
Her strong bag, and the stiff
Frost of her face (that challenges "When" and "If.")
And altogether she does Rather Well.

old tennis player

Refuses
To refuse the racket, to mutter No to the net.
He leans to life, conspires to give and get
Other serving yet.

a surrealist and Omega

Omega ran to witness him; beseeched;
Brought caution and carnality and cash.
She sauced him brownly, eating him
Under her fancy's finest Worcestershire.

He zigzagged.
He was a knotted hiss.
He was an insane hash
Of rebellious small strengths
And soft-mouthed mumbling weakness.

The art
Would not come right. That smear,
That yellow in the gray corner—
That was not right, he had not reached
The right, the careless flailed-out bleakness.

A god, a child.
He said he was most seriously amiss.

She had no purple or pearl to hang
About the neck of one a-wild.

A bantam beauty
Loving his ownhood for all it was worth.

Spaulding and François

There are cloudlets and things of cool silver in our dream, there
are all of the Things Ethereal.

There is a
Scent of wind cut with pine, a noise of
Wind tangled among bells. There is spiritual laughter
Too hushed to be gay, too high: the happiness
Of angels. And there are angels' eyes, soft,
Heavy with precious compulsion.

But the People
Will not let us alone; will not credit, condone
Art-loves that shun
Them (moderate Christians rotting in the sun.)

Big Bessie throws her son into the street

A day of sunny face and temper.
The winter trees
Are musical.

Bright lameness from my beautiful disease,
You have your destiny to chip and eat.

Be precise.
With something better than candles in the eyes.
(Candles are not enough.)

At the root of the will, a wild inflammable stuff.

New pioneer of days and ways, be gone.
Hunt out your own or make your own alone.

Go down the street.

About the author

About the book

Insights,
Interviews
& More ...

Read (and listen) on

Meet
Gwendolyn Brooks

I am interested in telling my particular truth as I have seen it.

—Gwendolyn Brooks

GWENDOLYN BROOKS wrote poetry for more than seventy years—poetry that consistently remained true to her unwavering commitment to lives actually lived, to her local and global communities, and to her poetic art. Her poetry underwent notable transitions, but in her passage from formal structures to free verse, from understated portraiture to outspoken militancy, she remained absolute in her artistry. She was, quite simply, a virtuoso of poetic technique. And through all those years, her major themes and concerns remained remarkably consistent: the details of day-to-day existence; the lives of "ordinary" people; the nature and consequences of racial and ethnic identity, and of prejudice; black pride and solidarity; family strengths and weaknesses; women's lives and loves; and the particulars of motherhood. Among her triumphs was her steadfast fidelity to the community in which she lived, worked, and taught. She found in the women, men, and children of America's black communities all that she

Bettmann/Corbis

needed to fill more than twenty books and to provide bountiful insight into lives everywhere.

Gwendolyn Elizabeth Brooks was born on June 7, 1917, in Topeka, Kansas. Five weeks later her parents—David Anderson Brooks, a janitor, and Keziah Corinne Wims Brooks, a schoolteacher—moved their family to Champlain Avenue in Chicago, where she would grow up within a tightly knit, loving family and a cheerful community. Her parents, she later reported, "subscribed to duty, decency, dignity, industry—*kindness*," a catalog of values that received repeated affirmation throughout Brooks's poetry. Reading and recitation were high-priority activities in the Brooks household.

An eleven-year-old Gwendolyn took her first firm step toward becoming Gwendolyn Brooks, poet, with the publication of four of her poems in a local newspaper, the *Hyde Parker*, followed by her first poem in a children's magazine called *American Childhood* at age thirteen. Three years later, she became a frequent contributor to the *Chicago Defender*, a newspaper produced primarily for Chicago's black community. She continued to write her poems through high school and while completing courses at Wilson Junior College. In a 1997 interview with B. Denise Hawkins in *Black Issues in Higher Education*, Brooks was asked what books she read when growing up. "When I was fifteen," she recalled, "I discovered a little book called *Caroling Dusk*. It featured the writings of poets like Langston Hughes and Sterling Brown. And the two Cotters—Joseph Cotter Senior and Junior." And she couldn't forget Paul Laurence Dunbar. "We had all of his books in the house," she told Hawkins, "and ▶

" [Brooks] found in the women, men, and children of America's black communities all that she needed to fill more than twenty books and to provide bountiful insight into lives everywhere. "

my father used to recite his works to my brother and myself. I told myself that if these people could write poetry and become famous, maybe I would also become famous one day. . . . I knew that I would write poetry always."

Brooks graduated from Wilson Junior College in 1936, in the depths of the Great Depression, and the only jobs she could find were domestic work, secretarial work for a spiritual advisor, and work on a women's magazine. At the age of twenty, she was publicity director of the Youth Council of the National Association for the Advancement of Colored People. In 1939 she married a young poet named Henry L. Blakely II. (They would have two children: Henry L. Blakely III and Nora.) In 1941 Brooks and her husband began attending a workshop in modern poetry at Chicago's South Side Community Art Center, sponsored by Inez Cunningham Stark, a reader for *Poetry*. Dedication and hard work, typical Brooksian virtues, paid off: After winning several local competitions and, in 1943, her first major award (at the Midwestern Writers' Conference), she was published in *Poetry* itself, that beacon of modern poetry.

Then, with Harper & Row's 1945 publication of her first volume, *A Street in Bronzeville,* Brooks became nationally known. What she preserved in the accomplished, mainly traditional structures of her early poems was the extraordinary quality of ordinary lives. Brooks would focus again and again on young people, with whom she empathized throughout her career. *A Street in Bronzeville* garnered favorable reviews and led to successive

> 66 Brooks graduated from Wilson Junior College in 1936, in the depths of the Great Depression, and the only jobs she could find were domestic work, secretarial work for a spiritual advisor, and work on a women's magazine. 99

Guggenheim fellowships in the two following years.

In addition to her first Guggenheim, 1946 also brought a National Institute of Arts and Letters grant in literature and an American Academy of Arts and Letters Award for creative writing. Brooks made good use of her fellowships and grants, working on the poems that appeared in her second collection, *Annie Allen* (1949). Adding the long mock epic, "The Anniad" to her triumphs in portraiture and vignette, *Annie Allen* received strong reviews. The *New York Times* praised it by saying, "When Miss Brooks . . . writes out of her heart, out of her rich and living background, out of her very real talent, then she induces almost unbearable excitement." The *Saturday Review* enthused, "She is a glory to read." In 1950 Brooks became the first black author to win the prestigious Pulitzer Prize in any category.

The Bean Eaters, Brooks's fifth publication, appeared in 1960, continuing her forthright, original studies of the lives mainly of poor urban blacks, but expanding her focus to take in the heroism of early civil rights workers and events of particular outrage. She dealt directly, for example, with the 1955 Emmett Till lynching and the 1957 school-desegregation crisis in Little Rock, Arkansas, placing "the evil that men do" within the commonplaces of the perpetrators'—and the victims'—everyday lives. *The Bean Eaters* consolidated Brooks's reputation as one of the nation's most admired poets.

Maud Martha, Brooks's only novel, was published by Harper & Row in 1953. In cumulative vignettes from a ghetto ▶

> In 1950 Brooks became the first black author to win the prestigious Pulitzer Prize in any category.

woman's life, Brooks presents the dark-skinned Maud's feelings of inferiority and her gradually acquired ability to insist on her own dignity in the face of disdain from within her own community, as well as outside it. Forty-four years later, *Newsday* called *Maud Martha* "a tough lyric jewel . . . as formidable an achievement as any of Brooks's poems. Or, for that matter, any work of fiction that came out of the 1950s." *Bronzeville Boys and Girls,* Brooks's first collection of poems for children, appeared next, in 1956.

By 1963 the civil rights movement was in full swing across the United States, and more and more black writers were increasingly outspoken in attacking American racism and insisting on full political, economic, and social equality for all black Americans. In that memorable year of the March on Washington, Harper & Row brought out Brooks's *Selected Poems,* which incorporated poems from her first three collections, as well as a selection of as-yet uncollected poems. The mid-1960s were years of awards, including the Robert F. Ferguson Memorial Award, the Friends of Literature award, and the Thormod Monsen Literature Award, via *Poetry.* Naturally, Brooks continued writing, teaching, giving readings, and promoting in every possible venue poetry's excitement and importance.

The Black Arts Movement also was powerful during these years. In the first volume of her autobiography, *Report from Part One* (1972), Brooks dated her own association with the movement, and its impact on her work, from the spring 1967 Fisk University Writer's Conference. The movement inspired a redefinition of herself

> ❝ The [Black Arts Movement] inspired a redefinition of [Brooks] and of her poetry. ❞

and of her poetry. She later said, in an interview for Claudia Tate's *Black Women Writers at Work,* that the black writers at the Fisk Conference "seemed proud and committed to their own people. . . . The poets among them felt that black poets should write as blacks, about blacks, and address themselves *to* blacks." Her work became more outspokenly militant, and she made greater use—with a technique as accomplished as ever—of free verse forms.

The first fruits of this new approach appeared in 1968, with *In the Mecca.* These poems display an intensified emphasis on the problems of racism and injustice. In a *New York Times Book Review* piece, Toni Cade Bambara noted in these and later poems "a new movement and energy, intensity, richness, power of statement and a new stripped, lean, compressed style." But despite the "raw power and roughness" that some reviewers ascribed to these poems, there is nothing bitter nor explicitly vengeful about the poems themselves. Brooks's poetry remained a poetry of clear vision, compassion, and artistic command.
In the Mecca, noted R. Baxter Miller in his book, *Black American Poets Between Worlds, 1940–1960,* "seeks to balance the sordid realities of urban life with an imaginative process of reconciliation and redemption." *In the Mecca* was nominated for the 1969 National Book Award, it received the 1968 Anisfield-Wolf Book Award (awarded annually to the year's best book on race relations), and Brooks was appointed the second Poet Laureate of Illinois, succeeding Carl Sandburg. ▶

" Brooks was appointed the second Poet Laureate of Illinois, succeeding Carl Sandburg. "

Meet Gwendolyn Brooks *(continued)*

The Black Arts Movement–related changes in Brooks's life and poetry also included her decision to leave her long-time publisher, Harper & Row, for the new Broadside Press, established in Detroit by Dudley Randall as one of several new publishing houses with the purpose of publishing black writers. Brooks's move to Broadside became effective in 1969, although Harper & Row would publish one more of her books in 1971, *The World of Gwendolyn Brooks,* which brought together in one volume her first four collections. When asked by B. Denise Hawkins why she left Harper & Row, Brooks replied that "Dudley Randall . . . was giving a platform to young Black poets, people that the larger publishers wouldn't accept. I thought it was the right thing for me to do. . . . I decided to go with a Black publisher and give some assistance to them."

Brooks's first volume with Broadside Press was *Riot,* in 1969, the same year in which the Gwendolyn Brooks Center for African American Literature was inaugurated at Western Illinois University, where Brooks had been teaching. *Riot* was inspired by the urban disorders following the assassination of Martin Luther King, Jr. Her later books with Broadside and Third World Press—*Family Pictures* (1970), *Aloneness* (1971), *Aurora* (1972), *Beckonings* (1975), *To Disembark* (1975), and *Winnie* (1988)—were, while remaining true to her artistic credo, contributions to the success of black publishers in the United States and to the continuing dialogue about racial equality and justice. Her poems, her teaching, and her workshops and readings also inspired a new generation of poets. Brooks once said, "My aim . . . is to write poems that will somehow successfully 'call' . . . all black people . . . in gutters, in schools, offices, factories, prisons, the consulate; I wish to reach black people in pulpits . . . in mines, on farms, on thrones." And she advised young poets, who flocked to hear her read, that it was crazy to walk in front of a firing squad: "Your effort should be in preventing the *formation* of a firing squad."

Brooks also edited several anthologies for Broadside Press, including *A Broadside Treasury* and *Jump Bad: A New Chicago Anthology,* both published in 1971. That same year she also received the Black Academy of Arts and Letters Award, for outstanding achievement in letters, and she was appointed Distinguished Professor of the Arts at City College of the City University of New York. The next year, 1972, brought *Aurora* and *Report from Part One: An Autobiography.* (*Report from Part Two* would be published in 1996.) Reviewers praised it for explaining Brooks's transformed perspective on her racial heritage and her responsibilities and role as a black poet.

During the last three decades of Brooks's life her poems, her children's books, her writing manuals for young poets, her teachings in the community, her honorary doctorates, and her numerous awards and appointments more than confirmed her importance and impact. "She makes them laugh, then leaves them staring in utter silence," reported the *Los Angeles Times* of a typical reading. In 1983 she became the first black woman elected an honorary fellow of the Modern Language ▶

'I wish to reach black people in pulpits . . . in mines, on farms, on thrones.'

Association. From 1985 to 1986, she served as the last consultant in poetry to the Library of Congress (after 1986 the honor was replaced by the annual appointment of a Poet Laureate of the United States). In 1988 she was inducted into the National Women's Hall of Fame and received the Essence Award. In 1989 she won the Poetry Society of America's Frost Medal and a Lifetime Achievement Award from the National Endowment for the Arts—followed, in 1990, by the University of Thessaloniki (Greece) Society for Literature Award (never before given to an American), and the Kuumba Liberation Award. More awards followed, leading to the next pinnacle of years, 1994–1995, when she was named by the National Endowment for the Humanities to give the Jefferson Lecture at the Kennedy Center, received the National Medal of Arts and the National Book Foundation medal for Lifetime Achievement, and had an elementary school in Aurora, Illinois, and a junior high school in Harvey, Illinois, named for her. Of course, she continued to gather well-deserved honorary degrees—more than seventy to date—from universities such as Duke, Northwestern, Howard, and the University of Illinois.

In awarding Brooks her 1996 honorary Doctor of Letters degree from The College of Wooster (Ohio), Wooster president R. Stanton Hales praised her "gifts of imagery and music," her unwavering devotion to racial justice, and her "celebration of the powers of endurance and creativity in us all." Whatever we consider to be the outstanding feature of her poetry— her "unsentimental regard and respect for all human beings" and her "whole gallery

66 [In the mid-1990s Brooks] had an elementary school . . . and a junior high school . . . named for her. 99

of wholly alive persons" (Janet Overmeyer, *Christian Science Monitor*), her "poised exactness" (David Littlejohn, *Black on White*), her capacity to present "all truth for the human condition wherever it is" (Blyden Jackson, *Black Poetry in America*), or her creation of "works of special encouragement to black writers and of enduring importance to all readers" (Reginald Gibbons, in *The Chicago Tribune Books*)—the final truth is that she remained true to her own vision and imagination, her virtuoso talent, and the truths of the men, women, and children (in Chicago, the nation, and the world) among whom she lived, for whom she wrote, and to whose lives she gave permanent grandeur. Like her old tennis player, she "leaned to life."

—*Hal Hager*

Remembering Gwen

by Nikki Giovanni

I AM 3,500 FEET ABOVE THE EARTH. It is autumn and quite beautiful. I am on my way to Chicago. Next to me, getting his pocket picked, is Ellis Haizlip. Why someone would try to pick a pocket on an airplane is beyond me but it is what we call *The Sixties*—though, in fact, it is now *The Seventies* and everyone is either dead or depressed so I guess people will try anything. Ellis turns to ask the woman if she is trying to pick his pocket. She is indignant. "Then what," he wants to know, "is your hand doing on my behind?" She sits way back. Now *he* is indignant. My sense of safety has now been breached. The plane hits a CAT, clear air turbulence.

The Granger Collection

I now accept the coming crash. I should never have even been on the plane. Ellis had called to ask if I could or would run over to Chicago with him. He is going to meet Gwendolyn Brooks.

"You don't need me to meet Gwendolyn Brooks," I point out.

"Yes," he insists, "I do. You have met her. You know all her friends. You are a militant, too. Things will go smoother if you go."

"Gwendolyn Brooks is not a militant. You don't need me."

"She has an Afro. She works with that gang, the Blackstone Rangers. She is dangerous."

"Don't be silly. She's a lovely old lady who will adore you. I'm sure she knows who you are."

"I don't want to go alone."

And that was that.

I had met Ms. Brooks when I was in college. She had come to Fisk University for a poetry reading and I was one of the people who was invited to the dinner. I didn't seriously think she had any reason to remember me, but Ellis was Ellis. He didn't want to go alone. I think the really stupid thing I said to Ms. Brooks was: "I wrote my seventh-grade book report on you and got an A." I don't honestly remember what she said in return, but the fact that she didn't sort of spit at my feet showed she was a real lady. "It's not as if she and I are friends, Ellis." But he didn't want to go alone.

We visited Gwen at her old homeplace on Cottage Grove. It was a small house with a fence, not picket, around it. She had invited some of OBACI to the encounter. Most of them I did know: Haki Madhubuti, Carolyn Rogers, and Walter Bradford, among others. We all sat in her living room in chairs or on the floor. She had made some snacks. I think Ellis wanted Gwen to appear on *Soul!*, which was the television show he hosted. The folk in the room kicked that one around, too. Gwen got up to clear away the dishes and I got up to help. I put what I was carrying in the sink then looked for the right door to open. "Which one is the dishwasher?" I asked, since I didn't want to appear meddlesome. "I don't have a dishwasher," she said. "But the dishes have to be done. Does Mr. Blakely do the dishes?" I was laughing then. "My Grandmother would never wash dishes. She said she cooked so Grandpapa had to do his ▶

share. I didn't know anyone else who did that!" I was enjoying sharing that bit of information. Gwen looked at me like I had lost at least half my mind. "I do the dishes," she said. "But why would you do that?" As if I had lost the other half she said very slowly, "Because—they—are—dirty." I have to tell you this: Yes. She washed them. But she refused to dry them. She put them away damp. "I never dry dishes because they will dry themselves. But I do wash them."

She was not a good cook either.

She didn't come to New York to do *Soul!* And *Soul!* at that time couldn't go to Chicago to film so it was our loss. Except that, for some reason, Gwen didn't think I was an idiot. I had written a thank-you note for our evening with her and enclosed my telephone number. I really couldn't think of a single thing a girl who'd had two books published could do for a Pulitzer Prize winner, but it was Grandmother's home training that came out. I didn't know then that Gwen was an early riser. And she liked to gossip. My phone would ring at 7:00 A.M. (6:00 A.M. CST) and she would say, as if I didn't know her voice, "It's Gwendolyn. Did I awaken you?" The answer to that is always "No," but Gwen's children were my age, grown and gone. My child was just out of diapers, so any sleep I could get was sorely welcomed. I would scuttle off to get a cup of coffee and see what the news was.

Peter Lawford was one of my favorite public figures, not only because he was in happy movies that I liked, but because when all was said and done he was the man who kept the secrets. I admire that.

> ❝ Gwen looked at me like I had lost at least half my mind. "I do the dishes," she said. ❞

14

Finally Gwen was going to Africa. I got an early morning call announcing the news. I sat right up. "How can that be!" I exclaimed. "There is no way they built a highway across the Atlantic Ocean!"

"Stop your caterwauling. I'm flying."

Gwen was noted for not flying. She and Mari Evans would take a train or bus or be driven. But to go to Africa you had to fly. Or cruise. And if one was scary the other was certainly unacceptable. What's the difference if you fall from the sky or fall into the ocean? She would fly.

She was going with her good friend Dudley Randall. When they got to New York we had dinner together. Gwen loved that Japanese restaurant that made the food at the table. Dudley mentioned that a larger company wanted to purchase Broadside Press. "Wow!" I said. "That's great news."

"I'm not going to sell," he said.

Gwen asked if I didn't agree. I didn't. "Sell and do something else. Sell and start a gallery. Sell and do whatever, but *Sell*. It's a business decision. Make it."

They both looked at me with that look. It was good advice. But no one listens to me. We had fun in New York, then they were off to Africa.

Gwen and I shared a birthday with Prince and Allen Iverson and a million other folk. Every year on June 7 I would open *USA Today* to the birthday notices. They would list everybody but Gwen and me. I finally wrote a blistering letter to the birthday editor: "I can see why you might not list me as I am not everyone's cup of tea, but what excuse do you have not to list Pulitzer Prize winner ▶

66 Gwen was noted for not flying. 99

66 Gwen and I shared a birthday with Prince and Allen Iverson and a million other folk. 99

15

Remembering Gwen *(continued)*

Gwendolyn Brooks, the poet laureate of
Illinois?" I CCed Gwen. In the next two
years our birthday fell on a Saturday, then
a Sunday. Then she died before she got to
see it.

Haki started a Gwendolyn Brooks Festival.
I was invited to the second or third one. Gwen
came in on Haki's arm in the most beautiful
pink St. John dress and Ferragamo shoes. I
went *Wow you look great!* "I spent too much
money," she said. *It's never too much when you
look this good.* She laughed. *Every
girl needs St. John.*

The last time I saw Gwen, Seattle was playing
the Bulls in Game Four. A group of us were
going to have dinner with her that night but
she didn't feel up to it. She invited us by for
dessert. When we arrived at the new home on
Chicago Beach Drive it was game time.

"Mind if we turn the game on?" we asked.

"Of course not," she said, "who's playing?"

"Gwen," I patiently began explaining, "this is
important. You must know basketball. How can
you be expected to be taken seriously as a black
woman if you don't know basketball?"

"I know Michael Jordan," she replied quite
huffily.

"Yes," I said, "but tonight we have to cheer for
Seattle."

"Oh, no. I can't cheer against Michael."

"Well, not against him," I tried to point out,
"but for Seattle, so that we can let Michael *really*
shine in Game Five."

When Michael Jordan gets the ball we raise
our hands and sway and say "Michael" in a sort
of chant.

"But tomorrow I can cheer for him?"

"Yes."

> " The last
> time I saw
> Gwen, Seattle
> was playing
> the Bulls in
> Game Four. "

When Mr. Blakely came in from his studio a bit later the four of us were engrossed in the game, chanting "Michael."

"How did you get my wife to watch the game, let alone cheer?" he asked, astonished.

"She likes me better than she likes you," I laughed. Of course he knew better.

Saturn had set up a "Thank-you" tour to acknowledge Black women for supporting their cars. It was a California-to-New York tour. Gwen was to join us in Chicago. Dr. B. J. Bolden took Gwen's place onstage. Then her cell phone rang. B.J. announced what we already knew.

Mr. Blakely died sitting in the same chair in which I sat when I last visited. He was watching a baseball game. I sent flowers to Mari Evans. People remember the family but forget what happens when you lose a friend. A meteor shot upward. There is a poem somewhere in the universe unread, unspoken, but most definitely felt. ∿

66 People remember the family but forget what happens when you lose a friend. A meteor shot upward. 99

Studs Terkel Interviews Gwendolyn Brooks, 1961

Broadcast on WFMT Chicago, January 3, 1961

[The interview commenced with Gwendolyn Brooks reading her poem "kitchenette building."]

That was "kitchenette building" (page 3, Selected Poems) as seen, observed if you will, poeticized by our guest, Gwendolyn Brooks, Pulitzer Prize winner living in Chicago. When we think of your poetry—and I suppose it's been described by many critics in so many different ways—but the honesty of it I suppose is the first word that comes to mind, the honesty and the simplicity of it. What do you feel when your poems are analyzed and criticized? What's your feeling?

Well, I read with great interest everything that's said. I myself have only tried to record life and interpret it as I have seen it.

As you have seen it. The poem we heard is from—was that your first volume of poetry, A Street in Bronzeville?

Yes, in 1945. . . .

We think of the title itself: A Street in Bronzeville. This would—what basically would you say? This is a poetic record of your observations of the community itself?

Yes, a record of my observations and, in some part, of my experiences. Certain things in all the books have happened to me or to people that I have known and—I've colored and interpreted as best I could.

What of you, the creative artist herself? We think of you as Chicago. Was it always Chicago?

Yes. I've always lived in Chicago. I was born in Topeka, but I prefer to think of myself as a Chicagoan because I was taken to Topeka to be born—if I may put it that way—and when I was a month old, well, my mother brought me back to Chicago and I have been here more or less ever since.

When was it poetry? The idea of poetry? The writing and reading of it? When did it come into your life?

My parents always saw to it that we had books in the house, and my mother took me to the library when I was about four or five. I enjoyed reading poetry and I tried to write it. I think I was about seven at the time that I first tried to put rhymes together, and I've loved it ever since.

In your childhood memories or later years, was there any one or any kind of poet who you feel had the most impact upon you?

In childhood years, I can't say. When I was twelve or thirteen I began to be interested in Shakespeare and poets such as Wordsworth and Tennyson and Shelley, the conventional loves of youth, I believe, and first loves, I ▶

❝ Certain things in all the books have happened to me or to people that I have known. ❞

Studs Terkel Interviews Gwendolyn Brooks, 1961 *(continued)*

should say, because I think we all still admire those poets.

If we may, I'm sure there will be a lot more questions that come to mind and from the audience as we hear you read some more work. We're with A Street in Bronzeville *and we wander along and on page nine there's "hunchback girl: she thinks of heaven."*

[Brooks reads "hunchback girl: she thinks of heaven" (page 5, *Selected Poems*).]

I suppose there can be no true poetry without compassion, without the understanding that you possess to such a degree, and again as we think of "hunchback girl," we think, I suppose of. . . . It's probing too much, isn't it, to think of your own observations of people you've seen?

No, it's not probing too much.

Well, I was thinking of the preacher coming up, which I would love to do, if I may.

Yes, I would like to hear you read.

[Terkel reads.]

What of the preacher that ruminates behind the sermon? This one?

Well, when I was younger—in fact, even to this day—I wondered and wonder what ministers in the pulpits are really thinking as they often say things that are rather conventional, sometimes cut and dried, and I've often wondered if they had any private feelings behind their words and that's why I wrote that poem.

Private worldly feelings, perhaps.

Yes, private worldly feelings, perhaps spiritual ideas other than those that they are giving us.

[Terkel reads "the preacher: ruminates behind the sermon" (page 8, *Selected Poems*).]

I suppose—with you as with any genuine poet, Gwendolyn—the matter of looking at people, into their souls, if you will, their thoughts as in that case. . . . I think of the poem on page three of A Street in Bronzeville: "the mother" *(page 4,* Selected Poems*). Anything you care to say about this? You don't have to if you don't want to. I know it's a poem that you feel strongly about.*

Yes. Once again I was trying to understand how people must feel—in this case a mother who never really became a mother. This poem was the only poem in the book that Richard Wright, who first looked at it, wanted to omit. He felt that a proper poem could not be written about abortions, but I felt otherwise and was glad that the publishers left it in.

At the time he wanted it omitted, but I'm wondering if in later years he would have felt that way about it? It's a conjecture of course. ▶

66 [Brooks's poem 'the mother'] was the only poem in the book that Richard Wright, who first looked at it, wanted to omit. He felt that a proper poem could not be written about abortions, but I felt otherwise. 99

Studs Terkel Interviews Gwendolyn Brooks, 1961 (*continued*)

I'd rather think he might have changed later.

[Brooks reads "the mother."]

Somehow, in thinking of "the mother," we think of the next poem too. You may read "the murder" on page twenty of A Street in Bronzeville. *And we think too of newspapers. When we think of newspaper reports of the coldness, the harshness in so many ways, the inhumanity of reports that deal with lives of people, events, I'm sure that the poem has found its way into news reports. I don't know what your basis was for writing it, but I'm sure there were many reports.*

Yes, "the murder" does have an interesting background.

Let's hear about "the murder."

This is something that happened in my own childhood right next door to me and on the street in Bronzeville. And there was only one difference: the mother was not gossiping down the street. She was working and the little boy really did keep asking when his brother was coming back. So I'll read it.

[Brooks reads "the murder."]

And so it seems putting into poetry that which you've seen and that which you've heard about isn't a question of calling upon your fantasy life but upon the actualities of your own.

Yes. That's what it has been. . . .

It seems, Gwendolyn, the whole world then is found in Bronzeville, whether it's "Matthew Cole" or "the event" or "the mother," or whether it's the girl I like whose song in the front yard. . . .

Well, that girl was me. My mother was very careful of her children, and at a certain time we had to come into the front yard and stay there. We couldn't go wandering down the block anymore. We used to envy the children who were free enough to do this. So I wrote.

[Brooks reads "a song in the front yard" (page 6, *Selected Poems*).]

Oh, Gwendolyn Brooks, what things you were telling us about yourself. And you were wondering at the beginning, you said you think you are inarticulate when it comes to. . . . Sometimes I am what is known as glib, but you are truly articulate in what you write and even in the things you say with such economy. Even now, I was thinking of this poem—your admiration for the rebel, too, is there. It seems to be there. . . .

Yes, I believe I do have such an admiration, in part at any rate.

[Brooks reads "The Rebel."]

So, we've been just hitting a few of the poems, touching on a few of the poems ▶

> “ That girl [in 'a song in the front yard'] was me. ”

Studs Terkel Interviews Gwendolyn Brooks, 1961 *(continued)*

from A Street in Bronzeville. *Then it was in 1949 that you wrote* Annie Allen.

Yes, it was published in 1949.

And this was the one that—it was the Pulitzer Prize winner for poetry in 1950. What would you say is the difference? Do you sense a difference in yourself, in your interest in the five years between A Street in Bronzeville *and* Annie Allen?

Yes, I think so. By the time I began to write *Annie Allen* I was very much impressed with the effectiveness of technique, and I wanted to write poetry that was honed to the last degree it could be. And I wanted chiseled wines, everything just right, real poetry I wanted to write, and that's the mood I was in when I began writing *Annie Allen.* I no longer feel that this is the proper attitude to have when you sit down to write poetry, but that's how I felt then.

You say you no longer feel it's the proper attitude to have when you write poetry? What do you feel now?

Well, I feel that my poems at any rate should be written more in the mood that I had when I wrote *A Street in Bronzeville.* I was just interested in putting people down on paper and, although it is rougher than *Annie Allen,* I feel that there's more humanity in it.

We'll come to your most recent work, The Bean Eaters, *later, and perhaps your feelings*

> " By the time I began to write *Annie Allen* I was very much impressed with the effectiveness of technique, and I wanted to write poetry that was honed to the last degree it could be. "

about that after we hear from **Annie Allen.**
*That won the big prize. There are sonnets
here from part three of* **Annie Allen,** *"The
Womanhood" (page 52,* **Selected Poems***). Is
there a reason for the division into sections
here?*

Yes, I was trying to trace the life of a young
woman and I thought it was convenient to
divide her . . . the first part of her life. I think
she must have been about twenty-eight when
the book ends.

*Before you read two of the verses from
"children of the poor" . . . you met some
of the poets who affected your very young
girlhood.*

When I was about nineteen or twenty I
became interested in the moderns, and I
admired and still do admire Eliot and John
Crowe Ransom, and a poet not spoken of
very much but whom I think is a wonderful
poet . . . Merrill Moore. He was a great
sonneteer. I think he died only a few years
ago. . . . He wrote thousands of sonnets.

*You mentioned sonnets. Here then, the sonnet
"the children of the poor" (page 52,* **Selected
Poems***).*

[Brooks reads "the children of the poor."]

Now "the rites for Cousin Vit" (page 58,
Selected Poems*). I know you chose this.
You like this very much. In reading it,* ▶

66 When I was
about nineteen or
twenty I became
interested in the
moderns, and I
admired and still
do admire Eliot
and John Crowe
Ransom. 99

Studs Terkel Interviews Gwendolyn Brooks, 1961 (*continued*)

I of course am crazy about it. What about "the rites for Cousin Vit"?

Well, that too is based on a real happening. Vit—of course that wasn't her name—was a friend of mine who had that irrepressibility that seems unconfinable even in death and that's why I wrote. . . .

[Brooks reads "the rites for Cousin Vit."]

Oh yes. Well, somehow in Cousin Vit I thought of Bessie Smith. Do you mind hearing this music played as a sort of commentary on your poems?

I was just thinking how effective the music is. It just seems inevitable.

In this, the irrepressibility, the irrepressibleness of your Cousin Vit . . . you might say Vit conquers death really. Is that what you're saying there?

In a way, yes.

And so we feel that about "Queen Bessie" too. There's old laughter opposite that, and this, I suppose, is a question of timelessness because, though you wrote this back in 1950. . . .

I didn't write this poem in 1950. I wrote it when I was about nineteen.

Oh, you did? I didn't realize that.

And, of course, I don't know anything about Africa. I have never been there, have never been that fortunate, but this is just a childhood impression that I had of Africa based on perhaps nothing.

Harper has always been your publisher, haven't they?

Yes.

The Bean Eaters *is available now.*

Yes. It was published in 1960. April.

And this is just a tip to the listeners who want a poetry that is poetry truly. **Bean Eaters.** *Before the book itself begins there's a dedication, Gwendolyn, "In Honor of David Anderson Brooks, My Father" (page 69,* **Selected Poems***). Anything you care to say about this dedication?*

Well, it doesn't have any reference to the book itself, but my father died just before the time that the book was about to be published and I naturally wanted to honor him in some way, so I quickly sent this poem to the publisher.

Was he an influence in some way?

Oh, my father was a wonderful man and he was devoted to poetry and music. He read a great deal and told my brother and myself stories from earliest childhood and sang to us wonderful ballads and read wonderful old poems. Plus, he had a tremendous influence on our lives. ▸

66 My father was a wonderful man and he was devoted to poetry and music. 99

27

Studs Terkel Interviews Gwendolyn Brooks, 1961 *(continued)*

[Brooks reads poem.]

Oh, how wonderful. [Reference to background music: "Deep River" sung by Roland Hayes.]

You said your father liked Roland Hayes.

Yes he did, and he would have been so happy to have heard that attached to . . . well, it's impossible, isn't it?

What of The Bean Eaters? *Is this a return to that humanity you felt was in* A Street in Bronzeville? *Less of the fineness of* Annie Allen. *You said something about this earlier.*

Yes, in a way, I think that's true. To tell you the truth, I haven't quite decided how I feel about this book yet. I myself enjoy *A Street in Bronzeville* more than any of them, but several people have said *The Bean Eaters* shows an advance and an interest in the quality of the human condition. I haven't quite decided yet.

Why The Bean Eaters? *What's the significance of the title?*

Well, I was referring to the great mass of eaters of beans, people who are not rich, who don't eat lobster as a rule but chiefly resort to beans.

"We Real Cool" on page seventeen (page 73, Selected Poems). There is a little note above the poem: "The Pool Players. Seven at the Golden Shovel."

Yes, it's about pool players.

There they were.

[Brooks reads "We Real Cool."]

Of course, I'm so taken with the rhythm of your reading. Would you mind telling us about that?

Well ideally, for myself at any rate, the "we" is supposed to be almost attached to the word that precedes it, and it's to indicate a sort of lost-ness and a sort of bewildered clutch at identity, a sort of—a little cry: *we.* And yet this "we" can't come and stand up straight and tall. . . . These pool players feel that way, although I'm sure that most of them wouldn't be able to express it.

What you have in this very brief poem . . . it has rhythm, too. Rhythm of them, the very rhythm, and at the same time what you're offering is their lost-ness. Sixty-two. Now we come to another aspect of Gwendolyn Brooks. It's part of a continuity, a very natural one. "The Ballad of Rudolph Reed" (page 110, Selected Poems). This is an actual event, isn't it? Would you mind. . . .

No, it's not an actual event.

Wasn't it?

No, this is pure imagination—of course based on things that have happened or can happen. ▶

66 ['We Real Cool' is] about pool players. 99

Studs Terkel Interviews Gwendolyn Brooks, 1961 *(continued)*

Oh, I thought there was a Rudolph Reed. This is pure imagination based upon some events similar to it.

Yes, for example—of course you can think of Trumbull Park, although I don't believe there were any deaths out there, but there could have been. That's what I meant.

Now you write this poem as almost a traditional child ballad, as a ballad, for the form itself is an old-time ballad form.

Yes.

May I try reading this?

Please.

[Terkel reads "The Ballad of Rudolph Reed."]

I was thinking, Gwendolyn, as I was reading this. . . .

And you read it very well.

Thank you. The power of this ballad—I think of . . . somehow the rhyme, the scheme . . . I think of "The Rime of the Ancient Mariner" and "Sir Patrick Spence." Have you heard of it?

I've heard of it. Yes.

As you wrote, did you have—aside from the content and the passion of it—were you thinking of old English ballads?

66 ['Rudolph Reed'] is almost a traditional child ballad. 99

No, not by this time. I have admired the ballad form for so many years. Once I get started, get a line, like "Rudolph Reed was oaken"—well, the rest just follows automatically. I love the ballad form.

"I am not hungry for berries. I am not hungry for bread, but hungry, hungry. . . . " Here is "Sir Patrick Spence," the old, old ballad. I think there's a form here that's similar to it, has that same power, like it's a through the ages feeling . . . if we may just hear of a piece of this.

[Terkel plays recording of "Sir Patrick Spence."]

Since you say this is based upon what might have been, there is a poem you hesitate to read—"A Bronzeville Mother Loiters in Mississippi. Meanwhile, a Mississippi Mother Burns Bacon." (page 75, Selected Poems)— because you heard Ruby Dee, that beautiful actress, read it on. . . .

Yes, a few months ago. She read it on a program, *Camera 3*, and she so beautifully translated my own thoughts that ever since I've rather hesitated to read it myself.

[Brooks reads the poem.]

I thought again that here, too, there's a reference made to a ballad. If we can perhaps open this with the name of the poem: "A ▶

Studs Terkel Interviews Gwendolyn Brooks, 1961 *(continued)*

Bronzeville Mother Loiters in Mississippi. Meanwhile, a Mississippi Mother Burns Bacon."

Well, the events in this poem are a little sturdier, I believe, than those in that beautiful ballad. They—it's the story, of course, of the murder of Emmett Till.

[Brooks reads "The Last Quatrain of the Ballad of Emmett Till" (page 81, *Selected Poems*).]

Imagine, Gwendolyn Brooks, your poem about this woman and about this man, about the boy who isn't there and yet is there, and about his mother who isn't there and yet is there says so much more than I imagine a tome or any kind of treatise on the subject could. Isn't this the poet's job? The poet gets to say what he wants to say pretty much.

Yes, to condense and to make concise, I believe. To refine.

To refine and to intensify. And these are but a few of the poems from The Bean Eaters *that are so beautiful and so eloquent. It's Harper & Brothers and it's available now. And perhaps to end this hour with you, Gwendolyn Brooks, the title poem itself. You spoke of the bean eaters being not the fine prince or the fine princess but so many of the people.*

[Brooks reads "The Bean Eaters" (page 72, *Selected Poems*).]

66 ['A Bronzeville Mother Loiters in Mississippi. Meanwhile, a Mississippi Mother Burns Bacon'] is the story, of course, of the murder of Emmett Till. 99

They have their own nobility too, a special kind. Gwendolyn Brooks, thank you very much for giving of your art, your reading, your poetry, your time.

Thank you.

The three books of Gwendolyn Brooks are A Street in Bronzeville, Annie Allen, *which won the Pulitzer Prize in 1950, and her new book, which a number of critics consider her finest, though you still lean toward* A Street in Bronzeville, *you yourself do.*

At present.

At present. Gwendolyn Brooks, thank you much indeed for being our guest.

Thank you. ∾

Reprinted by permission of the Chicago Historical Society

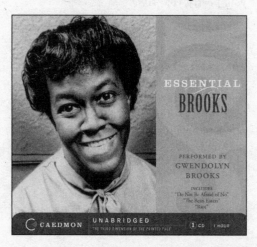